The Night Before Christian

JOY AVERY

THE NIGHT BEFORE CHRISTIAN

ISBN-13: 978-1522807971
ISBN-10: 1522807977

First Print Edition: December 2015

DEDICATION

Dedicated to the dream.

ALSO BY JOY AVERY

Smoke in the Citi
His Until Sunrise
Cupid's Error-a novella
His Ultimate Desire
One Delight Night
A Gentleman's Agreement

ACKNOWLEDGMENTS

My thanks—first and foremost—to God for blessing me with this gift of storytelling.

My endless gratitude to my husband and daughter for your unwavering support and patience. I love you both very much!

A huge thank you to my awesome critique partner, Lyla Dune.

To my friends and family who've offered tons and tons of encouragement and support, I express my greatest gratitude. Your support means the world to me.

To Angelia Vernon Menchan, THANK YOU!

Chapter 1

Clearly, the universe couldn't have cared less about Emory Chambers' aversion to being late. Evident by the fact there'd apparently been a power outage in her neighborhood, which reset her alarm. Batteries that should have prevented this from happening were so outdated they'd started to corrode. Then there was the little old lady she'd gotten stuck behind, who'd obviously believed if she drove faster than twenty miles per hour in a forty-five mile per hour zone, she'd be whisked into the future. And as if all of that hadn't been enough, every single traffic light on her route turned red the second she'd approached.

Now that she thought about it, the universe obviously had it out for her. Why? She had no idea. But if her morning foreshadowed how her day would go, she was in deep trouble. Maybe she should just turn around now, return home, and climb right back into her cold, lonely, empty bed.

Yeah, right. As if she had the luxury of turning down a new client. God, she was so tired of being a slave to the almighty dollar. Where was her tall, dark, handsome, filthy rich knight in shining armor sent to whisk her away from the life of a working woman? Actually, filthy rich wasn't a prerequisite, but it sure couldn't hurt.

"Dear Santa, how about sending Mr. Perfect-For-Me through my shop door today. I'll owe you big time. Plus, I've been a very good girl this year." She cringed. Well, if you didn't count the time she slammed the door in the face of the pigtail wearing Girl Scout cookie peddler. That had been justified. The child had tried to entice her with Lemonades. Who could resist *Lemonades*?

Hopefully, the fact Emory had chased pigtails down and purchased six boxes of the addictive cookies redeemed her. She doubted Santa even answered thirty-four-year-olds, anyway. But just in case… It couldn't hurt to put it out there.

The sound of the car horn blaring behind her snatched Emory back to reality. Pulling away from the green light, she ogled her favorite coffee spot, Pour Play Coffee Bar. A huge mug of coffee was just what she needed. Scratch that. She needed a five-gallon bucket filled to the brim. *Strong and black*. She was about to tell Santa it was exactly how she wanted her man, but it was Santa, which meant he already knew that.

Ugh. She pressed the pedal down a little harder. Stopping would only put her further behind schedule. When her Honda Accord backfired, spitting out a cloud of black smoke, she was sure she'd have to hoof it the remainder of the way. Did everything in her life have to go wrong all at once?

At least there was one good thing about her crappy day, all of the Christmas decorations throughout downtown Raleigh. Just the sight of wreaths hung from street lamps, garland and lights arranged in store fronts, and the continuous Christmas music on the radio thrilled her. Christmas had always been her favorite time of the year, but she was having trouble getting into the holiday spirit.

Finally arriving at her flower shop, The Bloom Bloom Room, on luck and a prayer, she parked the heap, bolted from the vehicle, and stumbled through the backdoor. When her purse hit the floor, the stack of overdue bills spilled out. The last thing she needed was a reminder that she was sinking in debt. *And going down fast.* Refusing to linger on the idea, she collected them and stuffed them back inside.

Lucas, her trusty assistant, exited from the small office to her right. He ran his long fingers through his dusty blonde hair. "*Crikey!* It sounded like a mob of roo were bursting through the door. Are you okay?" he asked, his Australian accent as thick as if he'd stepped off the plane from Sydney just yesterday.

"Rough, *rough* morning. But, hey, it's almost Christmas. This day *has* to get better, right?"

In true Lucas fashion, he lifted a cream colored carnation off one of the work tables, snipped it, and placed it behind her ear. "She'll be right."

Emory understood the phrase was Australian for *it will be okay*. Call her a pessimist, because she wasn't sure it would be. But at least one of them held out hope. "Thank you for calling me this morning. If you hadn't, I'd probably still be asleep."

"You needed the rest."

She agreed one hundred and ten percent. Ever since her quaint North Carolina shop was featured in Floral Trendsetters Magazine, business had been booming. Or *blooming* as Lucas liked to say. God, she would miss him when he left for a month-long trip to Australia in a few days.

"On a scale of one to ten, how annoyed is Ms. Manchester?" The hopefully tolerant bride who'd been waiting close to a half-hour for her.

"You're the most sought after florist in Raleigh. She can wait." He winked. "Go get 'em tiger."

Emory laughed at Lucas' terminology. "You are the absolute best, Lucas. If you weren't already married, I'd propose."

Lucas pressed a finger into his chin and eyed the ceiling. "Let me think about this. That's a tempting offer."

Emory laughed because she knew it would take a force far more powerful than any woman possessed to snag Lucas from his wife. She'd never witnessed a couple more in love. She'd never known a man who

cherished a woman like Lucas cherished his. Actually...
she had. *Once*.

Shaking away the memory of her ex, Emory moved
through the door and entered the large room she used
for consultations. Pasting on a two dollar smile, she
said, "Ms. Manchester?"

The woman stood, extending her arm. "Please, call
me Yasmin. And thank you so much for seeing me on
such short notice."

Yasmin was dressed in a winter white pantsuit,
makeup flawless, and not a hair out of place in the tight
bun she sported. This made Emory wish she'd put a
little more effort into her own appearance. But she'd
worn the possibly-too-snug tee and jeans for comfort,
not fashion. "It's not a problem at all. I apologize for
being late. It's been an insane morning."

"Trust me, I understand."

Yasmin smiled, revealing the most perfect set of
teeth Emory had ever seen. So perfect, in fact, she
questioned to herself whether or not they were even
real.

Yasmin gracefully took a seat. "My fiancé will be
joining us any moment."

"Wonderful." In her experience, not many men
chose to be involved in the selection of the wedding
flowers. It would actually be refreshing having the
groom present to get his input. "My assistant will show
him in when he arrives. Would you like to wait for him
before we get started?"

Yasmin checked her watch, a Rolex studded with

diamonds. "No. He's just here for moral support. He knows I'll have the final say."

That was typically how it went. The bride dragged the groom along under the pretense that he would have a say-so in the details. And on the off chance he'd gotten to make a decision, by the end of the consultation, the bride would have already overridden him. Unless, of course, it was exactly what she'd wanted from the beginning. A well-informed groom knew to smile, nod, and supply the occasional yes.

Emory removed her checklist and asked Yasmin a multitude of questions, in an attempt to get an idea of what she had in mind for her special day. Did she want traditional Christmas themed or something out of the box? Simple and elegant or over the top lavish?

Yasmin flashed a palm. "I really haven't put much thought into any of this. We were just engaged three months ago." She flashed a ring that should have come with protective eyewear.

"Wow! That's some ring." The center stone alone had to be at least five-carats. The baguettes only added to the gaudy piece.

"My mother suggested I hire a wedding planner. I think I will be taking her advice. Especially since I have to fly out of the country today for a three-week-long modeling gig. I haven't even put a dent in my to-do list. Silly me. I'd convinced myself I could handle it all by myself."

It made sense that she was a model: tall, thin, and a picture of perfection—by society's standards—but flying out of the country for three weeks with an impending wedding... That was just plain ridiculous. "Yeah, you're going to need a planner. I can give you a referral."

Newly engaged. A rushed wedding. Emory's first thought was that the woman was pregnant and wanted to tie the knot before she started to show. Well, if nothing else, the flowers would be breathtaking.

"Oh, a referral would be great. My fiancé and I recently moved to North Carolina. He's originally from here, but I'm not. I know absolutely no one here. So, I'm looking for all the help I can get. I would have preferred a destination wedding. Hawaii, maybe. But our families..."

She smiled, but Emory noted it lacked a lot of the glow she typically witnessed in her brides.

"Is it odd that I'm not over the top elated about my wedding? I mean... I'm getting married in a few weeks. Shouldn't I be over the top?"

"You will be. Right now, you're just overwhelmed. Once everything comes together, you'll be ecstatic."

Emory had witnessed brides with cold feet before, but this was something more. This was uncertainty. Did Yasmin harbor second thoughts about getting married?

"It's just that..." She shook off whatever thought she'd been crafting in her head. "Yeah, I guess you're right." Yasmin flailed her hands. "Anyway. Help. Please. Just make it gorgeous."

"That, I can definitely do." Emory loved when she got free reign to do whatever she liked. Within budget, of course. And speaking of budget… "Is there a specific—?"

When three light taps sounded behind them, Emory tossed a glance over her shoulder. Lucas stood at the door.

"The groom is here," he said, stepping aside. "And I'm going to run out for a bit. I'll be back shortly."

Emory nodded, but froze a second later. Were her eyes playing tricks on her? She blinked a couple of times to make sure she wasn't seeing things.

"I apologize for my tardiness. I've had the worst day known—"

Obviously, familiarity set in, because Yasmin's fiancé stopped mid-thought. The room went still. Or least it did for Emory. Her mouth went dry and her heart rapped in her chest with such force she thought it would stop from overload. When she'd asked Santa to send a man through her door, she hadn't meant this one. Old Saint Nick obviously had a sense of humor.

"—to man," he continued.

Clearly, he was as stunned by her presence as she was of his. Yasmin rounded the table to greet him with a hug and peck on the lips.

"Honey, this is floral designer extraordinaire, Emory Chambers. Emory, this is my fiancé…

Christian St.Clair, Emory said along with Yasmin, but only in her head.

Yasmin's cell phone chimed. "Excuse me a moment."

Yasmin stepped away, leaving the two of them in

an awkward space together. The air grew so thick, Emory found it difficult to pull in a breath. Or it could have been the fact that she was too stunned to process the command.

Emory had imagined what she'd do if she ever saw her ex again. Paralysis hadn't been one of the scenarios crafted in her head. On the sporadic occasions her thoughts drifted to him over the years, she'd visualized him a hundred pounds heavier, a receding hairline, a potbelly, and missing teeth. That was so *not* the man standing in front of her now.

Even beneath the black wool trench coat, she could see that his body was still as solid as it'd been the last time they'd been in the same room together. Approximately two years ago, she noted. Suddenly, the snug shirt she wore became uncomfortably warm.

The frown stretched across his face suggested he was far from happy to see her. Understandable. He'd probably spent the past two years hating her. Understandable, as well.

Steadying her frayed nerves, Emory stood, extended her hand, and said, "Nice to meet you, Christian," before he did something ridiculous like reveal to his wife-to-be that they'd know one another once. Actually, they'd more than known one another; they'd planned a life together. One that she'd shredded.

When Christian hesitantly gripped her hand, she hoped he hadn't noticed the tremble in it. It'd been so long since they'd touched, but his hold on her—warm and firm—was familiar. Too familiar. Locked onto his

11

gaze, her stomach fluttered. Those eyes—deep, dark, commanding—teased her now just as they'd done in the past. It was a damn good thing Yasmin was preoccupied with her cell phone, because if she'd witnessed their exchange, there'd be some 'plaining to do.

Emory reclaimed her hand, Christian's heat still present in her palm. "Shall we continue?" she said, snatching her focus away from him.

Christian eased into the chair directly across from her, his seething gaze threatening to send them all up in a raging ball of fire. It wasn't difficult to ascertain he wasn't overly thrilled to be there, but that was okay because she wasn't too keen on him being there either.

Though she'd avoided eye contact with him, his mere presence threw her off her usually flawless game. Words that usually flowed, she stumbled over. Phrases that normally came second nature, she forgot. And the sweating. She perspired like she'd been perched on a bed of burning coals.

Getting through the remainder of the consultation proved one of the toughest challenges Emory had ever faced. Luckily, Christian hadn't added a great deal to the conversation, which limited their need to address one another. But every time she dared a glance in his direction, his eyes were steadied on her—hard and cold.

Never in her life had she been so happy to see a couple leave as she'd been when Christian and Yasmin departed. The entire encounter had drained her. She rested her head on the chilly conference room table and closed her eyes. How was it possible that Christian could still rattle her system this way?

He sure wore thirty-seven well. Why did he have to look so damn delicious? And the way he wore that custom-tailored suit. It should have been a crime against humanity. No one should look that damn delectable in fabric. Plus, those muscles. How was it possible for his body to have improved? It'd been pristine when they were together. It was downright lethal now. Muscle on top of muscle, powerful legs, a tight ass, and—

She groaned. Was she insane? This man was about to become someone else's husband. But could she actually watch it happen? Maybe passing on this event would be a smart thing to do.

Instantly, the six thousand dollar bill from her mother's homecare agency played in her head, reminding her of why she didn't have the option of passing up any business.

The sound of the conference room door opening, then slamming behind her drew her urgent attention. When she glanced up, Christian hovered over her like a sexy, simmering god. A vein bulged on the side of his neck, and she added *vengeful* to the list.

"What in the hell do you think you're doing?" he asked.

Something told her this would not be a pleasant encounter. Maybe it was his darkened eyes. Or his flared nostrils. Or the proverbial smoke wafting from his ears. *Play it cool, Emory. Don't let him see you sweat—well, sweat anymore. And whatever you do, keep your emotions in check.* "Christian—?" That was all he gave her time to release.

"You will call Yasmin and tell her something urgent has come up... Death in the family, the flu, I don't care. Just as long as she knows you *will not* be involved in our w—" He paused, his jaw muscles flexing, then relaxing, then flexing again. "You'll do it today." Each word he spoke was taut and exact.

Something about his authoritative tone corrupted her thoughts of them actually having a cordial conservation. He—of all people—knew she didn't take orders. Especially from him. Emory bolted to her feet. "Who in the hell do you think you're talking to? Your *fiancée* hired me to do a job, and I damn sure intend to do it." So much for keeping her emotions in check.

"Over my dead body."

"That can be arranged."

He ground his teeth so hard she thought his jaw would snap out of place. A beat later, he released a sound that could be construed as more of a mock than jovial laughter.

"Not everyone's a big time aerospace engineer. Some of us need the money because—" She stopped abruptly, breaking off the string of words before revealing too much. He wouldn't care that her mother's health issues were sending her to the poor house. He simply wanted his way.

"Is that what this is all about? You're hard up for a

dollar?" He reached into his pocket, removed his wallet, snatched all of the bills from inside and tossed them onto the table. "There you go."

Twenty dollar bills scattered over the dark wood. His actions infuriated her so much a bout of nausea washed over her. Why did everyone in this family believe she could be bought? Even if she were contemplating quitting before, there was no way she would now. Staring him square in the eyes, she said, "You're going to need far more than that to cover my bill. And I'm not quitting."

A vein pulsed in the center of his forehead. "Like hell you're not."

Who was this man who stood in front of her? This hardened shell was not the warm and loving Christian St. Claire she once knew. He turned to leave, but she wasn't going to allow him the last word. "When did you become such a heartless bastard?"

Christian stopped mid-reach of the doorknob. His body tensed and he seemed to struggle with whatever thoughts raced through his head. Over his shoulder, he finally said, "When the only woman I've ever loved spit that love back in my face and showed me she never truly cared for me at all."

He was never one for hiding his true feelings from her. A beat later, Christian yanked the door open with so much force Emory swore it would come off the hinges. Though his words briefly froze Emory, awareness returned before Christian escaped.

"Oh no, you don't." She slammed her hand into

the door and banged it shut. Under any other circumstances, being this close to the man who'd taken her body to places she could only label as uncharted territory would have rendered her unable to speak. But with the degree of anger coursing through her, the words came readily. "How dare you say that to me? That's bullshit and you know it. I've always loved you. I've never *not* loved you. What I did then, I did for—" She stopped abruptly. Calming her tone, she said, "You don't know everything, Christian."

His shoulders slumped and eyes grew weary. "I know I loved you. I know I loved you more than I loved myself. I know my life was supposed to have been with you. I know you walked away and never looked back. I know that now I'm doing the same."

As bad as she wanted to wrap her arms around him, tell him she'd loved him with the same intensity— still loved him—she couldn't. Swallowing the painful lump of emotion in her throat, she repeated, "You don't know everything."

Through clinched teeth, he said, "I know enough." Staring into her eyes, he said, "Stay away from me, Emory."

His words cut her to the core, but the hurt, the pain, the torture she witnessed in his eyes told her it was useless to say any more. She stepped aside and allowed him to exit. What was the benefit in telling him that just because she'd let him go, didn't mean she'd wanted to, or that she'd walked away to protect him and the only life he'd ever known.

Goodbye, Christian.

She never imagined she'd be uttering those painful words again in this lifetime. He bolted through the shop door without as much as a glance back in her direction.

Emory fell against the doorjamb. How could he not believe she'd ever loved him?

"You're wrong," she mumbled. "You're so wrong."

She'd displayed unconditional love in its purest form—sacrifice.

Chapter 2

From the second Christian entered his brother's place—
ten minutes—ago, he'd paced the floor. Why in the hell
was he letting his encounter with Emory get to him?
She was his past. A past that'd come to a screeching
halt with no more than an "*I need space*" as an
explanation.

He couldn't shake her from his thoughts, or what
she'd said. *"You don't know everything?"* The words had
bounced around in his head since he'd left her shop.
What didn't he know? *It doesn't matter*. At least, he
was damn sure trying to convince himself it didn't.

Of all the flower shops in Raleigh, how in the hell
had he walked into Emory's? The moment had played
out just like a movie. Their eyes locking, both
bewildered, neither able to turn away. And the
attraction… His attraction to her had been off the chart.
Clearly, his body had no qualms about betraying him.

She'd looked good. Damn good. Swearing under his breath, he cursed himself for even allowing such thoughts to materialize. He didn't want to think about how damn good she looked. He didn't want to think about how damn nice she smelled. He didn't want to think about her period, dammit.

Floral designer extraordinaire? When in the hell had she taken an interest in floral design? Giving it some thought, they hadn't spoken in years. He was sure she'd developed an array of new interests.

"Christian, man, please sit down. You're giving me motion sickness," his younger brother Chauncey said.

Christian massaged the stiffness in his neck. "Can you believe she had the audacity to tell me she wasn't quitting? Like she has a damn choice," he said more to himself than Chauncey.

"Come on. You, of all people, should know how headstrong Emory is. And the harder you push…"

Chauncey was right. She was as stubborn as a constipated mule. That was one of the many reasons he'd fallen in love with her. She never took shit from anyone. Including him. Especially him. That definitely hadn't changed. At least, the taking shit from him part.

Chauncey fell back against the cushion of the chair he occupied. "Cut her some slack. She's had a rough year."

This slowed Christian's steps, the words fully garnering his attention. "Rough year? What happened? What's going on? Is everything all right?" He stunned himself with the amount of concern present in his voice.

"Damn. Take a breath," Chauncey said with mock humor in his tone.

Christian shot him the bird. When the laughter settled, Chauncey's expression turned serious. Whatever had his brother so bothered wasn't good.

"Her mother's Alzheimer's Disease is progressing. It's taking a toll on Emory."

Fine lines etched across Christian's forehead. "Alzheimer's? When was Ms. Anne diagnosed with Alzheimer's?"

"Like two years ago I believe. You didn't know?"

Christian dropped into the sofa across from his brother. "No, I didn't." *Alzheimer's*? He'd seen the devastation of this condition up close and personal. His grandfather had succumbed to the effects of the dreaded disease. Ms. Anne's diagnoses had to have come after he and Emory had broken up. *Damn. Not Ms. Anne*. He'd loved that lady. "Emory has to be taking this hard. They were really close."

Chauncey nodded. "She is. She refuses to put her mother in a facility. She wants to keep her in familiar surroundings."

Christian kneaded at the tension in the crook of his neck. "That doesn't surprise me."

"She's also footing the bill for her mother's place and 'round the clock care."

That didn't surprise him either. "How do you know all of this?" Better yet, why hadn't he shared any of this with him before now? Then it hit him. Chauncey probably thought he was sparing him by not bringing

Emory up. It'd been a good call.

Chauncey smirked. "I keep my ear to the ground."

By looking at Emory, Christian wouldn't have known all she was going through. As always, she was a picture of perfection. This had to be hell for her. For a brief moment, it angered Christian that Chauncey knew more about Emory's life than he did. But once the sentiment passed, he reminded himself that these weren't his burdens to bear. Emory was no longer a part of his life. Well…a part of his intimate life.

Chauncey cuffed his hands in front of him. "She came close to losing her shop a few months back. Taking care of two households and helping to put her sister through college… It's draining her. I offered to help, but of course she turned me down. She said she don't take handouts, then promptly told me to stay the hell out of her business."

Christian chuckled. Yep, that was Emory. Strong-willed and stubborn. Trying not to appear overly interested, he said, "I'm guessing she found a way to save her shop. Seeing how she's taunting me from it."

"For now, at least. Some floral design magazine did a piece on her. She got a boost in business from the article. It was a nice write-up, too." He pointed over his shoulder. "I might have a copy if you want to read it."

Christian scrubbed his hand down his face, ignoring the taunt in Chauncey's words. "I'm good."

Now he understood why she'd refused to step away. She needed the income. He thought about the comment she'd cutoff about needing money. As hard as he fought it, regret flooded him. The way he'd treated her gnawed at him with razor-sharp teeth. Her sad brown eyes staring up at him haunted his thoughts. *Damn*. Why'd he have to be such an *asshole* to her?

"It must have been one hell of a shock walking into the room and seeing Emory sitting there."

A shock? That would be the understatement of the year. Plus, it didn't come close to what he'd felt—anger, confusion, anxiety. Yet, through all of those negative emotions, he'd also felt a sense of calm he hadn't experienced in so long. Standing so close to Emory, his body had done things that no soon-to-be married man's body should have done for any woman other than his fiancée.

Scattering the troubling thoughts, he refocused on their conversation. "Let's just say it took me by surprise." One helluva surprise.

Chauncey lifted his beer from the table and took a swig. "Just in case you're wondering, she's single. Never could replace you, I suppose."

When Chauncey smirked, Christian tossed one of the red holiday pillows at him. "Go to hell." Christian laughed along with his brother, but his thoughts lingered on what Chauncey had just said. *Still single*? Why hadn't someone snatched Emory off the market?

A silence fell between them, allowing a hard dose of reality to settle into Christian's head. "I'm getting married," he said. Why in the hell did the thought knot his stomach into a painful ball? Shouldn't he be floating or something?

Chauncey inched to the edge of his chair, rested his elbows on his thighs, and cupped his hands in front of him. The move signaled deep conversation would follow. "It's just the two of us here, bro. What's said doesn't leave this room."

Christian studied the serious expression on his brother's face, then nodded. "Go 'head."

"If Yasmin hadn't gotten pregnant, would you have proposed to her?"

Christian reclined against the plush cushion and hugged an identical red pillow to his chest. "I'm a St. Claire. St. Claire men don't run away from their responsibilities." Unless of course you were their father.

Chauncey barked a laugh. "That sounds like some shit Matriarch would say."

Matriarch was the name Chauncey affectionately called their grandmother behind her back. If the stern woman had any idea, she'd probably cut him from her will. She wasn't beyond trying to control people with money. And that included her grandsons.

"I did what I thought was the right thing to do," Christian said.

"So, that's a no."

Christian shot him a scowl. "She was carrying my child. I didn't want to be like our father and leave his kids to—" He stopped abruptly, remembering how sensitive Chauncey got when it came to their part-time—make that their *no-time*—father. "Anyway, I did what I felt needed to be done. After the miscarriage..." His words trailed off.

23

Even though he hadn't planned on Yasmin getting pregnant, he'd truly started to welcome the idea of becoming a father. Then the accident. Christian's heart ached at the memory. How life could change in the blink of an eye.

"Do you love, Yasmin, bro? Truly love her. The way you and I know a man should love the woman he's intending to spend the rest of his life with. Do you love her the way you loved Emory?"

There was no woman alive he could love the way he'd loved Emory—or would dare to love the way he'd loved her. "Don't do that psychology shit on me. And don't try to give Emory any shares of my heart. At one time, she owned the majority, remember? She cashed them in when she—" He pushed to his feet, his anger swelling. Why in the hell did Emory's dumping him still get such a rise out of him? "I need another beer," he said, despite not having finished the first.

Chauncey trailed him into the kitchen. "Don't marry this woman, Christian. Not if you don't love her. And definitely don't marry her because Matriarch says it's what you should do."

"Grandmother has nothing to do with this. I'm my own damn man." He slung the fridge door open. "I care about Yasmin."

"You *care* about Yasmin? Bro, this is the woman you're about to pledge the rest of your life to. You need to do more than care about her."

Christian rolled his eyes away from Chauncey and rummaged inside the refrigerator. Chauncey wasn't telling him anything he hadn't considered himself.

"Considering the degree of concern you showed a moment ago, I have to ask... Are you still in love with Emory?"

Christian whipped toward Chauncey. "Why in the hell would you ask me something so comical?"

"Comical? Funny, I don't hear you laughing."

"*Ha, ha.*"

Chauncey continued to rouse him, but Christian paid him no attention.

"This is me you're talking to. Admit it. You're still in love with Emory."

Christian sighed heavily, then slammed the fridge door. Brushing past Chauncey, he said, "I'm going home. Call me when you get some damn sense."

"Oh, I'm not the one who needs to get some damn sense. I'm not the one in denial. Just admit the obvious. You're still in love with the one who got away."

Christian whirled around. "Yes, dammit. I'm still in love with her. You happy now?"

Chauncey rested a hand on Christian's shoulder. "No. I'll be happy when you decide not to make the biggest mistake of your life by marrying the wrong woman."

Christian snatched up his coat. "Well, if Emory were the *right* woman...she'd be the one I was marrying, wouldn't she?" He started for the door. "I guess you should get used to being unhappy, because I'm marrying Yasmin."

***

Emory yanked up another ornament and haphazardly placed it onto a limb of the artificial Noble Fir Christmas tree. A second later, the glass bulb tumbled to the floor, shattering. "Damn."

"Okay. What's up with you, Em?" her sister Jordyn asked, using the nickname she'd given her when she was younger. "You're normally ecstatic about decorating for Christmas. That's the third bulb that's met its fate in your hands."

"Nothing," she snapped.

"Well, excuse me."

Emory closed her eyes and rested her hand over her forehead. After releasing an exasperated sigh, she turned to Jordyn. "I'm sorry. It's been a tough day."

"Want to talk about it?"

Did she really want to relive her confrontation with Christian? The thought of rehashing it made her temple throb. "No. Really I don't."

But in true Jordyn fashion, she didn't take no for an answer. "You know what mommy used to say about keeping things bottled up."

"*Things burst under pressure*," they said in unison.

Emory studied Jordyn a moment. "Christian came by the shop today."

Jordyn squealed. "I knew it. I knew it. I knew you two would find your way back to each other. And at Christmas. How romantic is that?" She gazed off starry-eyed. Refocusing, she said, "Tell me everything. Every single detail. Did he confess his undying love for you? Did you confess yours for him?"

If either of those things had happened, did Jordyn really think she'd be here decorating a tree? "He's getting married." The words left a sour taste in her mouth.

Jordyn sobered quickly. "What do you mean he's getting married?"

"A bride. A groom. A church. I do."

"What the hell, Emory?"

"*Shh*," Emory hissed, "before you wake mom."

They both glanced down the hall in the direction of their mother's bedroom.

Jordyn dismissed her warning with a swipe of the hand. "He can't marry someone else. He's yours."

Jordyn was wrong. He wasn't hers any longer. And his presence in her shop cruelly reminded her of that fact. "He can and he will. In a few weeks. And guess who's doing the flowers?" She flashed a tight smile. "Me."

Jordyn's eyes widened. "You're shittin' me."

"Watch your mouth."

"Are you freaking insane? You can't do the flowers for this wedding. You're in love with the groom. Oh, this is bad. This is really bad." Pity gleamed in Jordyn's usually playful brown eyes. "Are you okay?"

"Of course I'm okay. And for the record, I'm not in love with the groom. What we shared was over a long time ago. I'm happy for him and wish them both the best. He's marrying a lovely lady whom he seems to care for very much." Emory's chest tightened. God, she really wanted to mean what she'd said—the part about her being happy for him—but she wasn't so sure she was.

"I don't care what you say. I'm not allowing you to do it."

Emory rested a hand on her hip. "Uh, who is the older sister here? And have you forgotten about mom's medical bills?" she said in a hushed tone. "I don't really have a choice. We need the money."

"I told you I would quit school and get a job to help out."

"And I told you no."

"But—"

"Absolutely not, Jordyn." Emory closed her eyes and took a deep breath. "Look, I know you're worried about me, but I'm fine. We're fine. Everything is fine."

"And Christian getting married... Is that fine, too?"

Emory sighed heavily. "It's been two years. I'm over Christian St. Claire. He's moved on and so have I. So, yes, it's fine." She returned to placing ornaments. "Fine, fine, fine."

Jordyn tilted her head. "Moved on? Really? You haven't been on a date since the two of you broke up. *Two years* without getting your—"

Emory pointed a gingerbread ornament at her sister before the rest of the sentence escaped. "Watch your mouth," she said, because knowing her sister, something inappropriate was sure to follow. "I haven't been on a date because I don't have time to date. I'm too busy keeping your fast behind out of trouble."

Jordyn pressed her manicured fingers into her chest. "Who me?" She batted her eyes. "I'm an angel." Holding a tinsel covered ring above her head, she said, "See, I even have a halo."

They shared a dose of much needed laugher.

Jordyn draped her arms around Emory. "Are you sure you're going to be all right?"

Emory cradled her in an affectionate embrace. "Yes, I'll be fine. Promise." But honestly, she wasn't so sure.

Even though she'd told Jordyn she no longer loved Christian, truthfully, she'd never stopped loving him. In fact, she still loved him like they'd never spent one day apart. And his presence in her shop earlier only intensified the sentiment. But he'd made it perfectly clear that she was the very last thing on his mind.

Getting through this event would be the hardest thing she'd ever had to do, but she *would* do it. She *had* to do it. And not just for herself. For everyone depending on her. For everyone she loved. Maybe this was just what she needed to finally purge Christian from her system once and for all.

"Emory, baby?"

Emory turned to see her mother shuffling down the hall, her frail body a potent reminder of what the once vibrant woman was going through. *Second hardest thing*, she corrected. "Mom, what are you doing out of bed?"

Her mother's eyes scanned the room. "Baby,

29

where's your father? He was supposed to be home from the factory hours ago. I hope every things okay."

A worried expression spread across her mother's face. Emory's heart broke a little more every time she had to deliver the same devastating news. Maybe Jordyn had seen the pain in her eyes, because she stepped in.

"Mommy, daddy died, remember?"

"Died?" Their mother rested a hand over her collarbone and rubbed frantically. "Oh, Lord, Jesus. My Larry died. I have to see him. I have to see my Larry."

Jordyn took her mother's hand. "Mommy, daddy died six years ago."

"And nobody told me. Why didn't anybody tell me my Larry was gone?"

When Emory tried to cradle the agitated woman, she swatted her away. There were good days and there were bad days. Today was clearly the latter. "Calm down, Mom. Please." Her voice cracked with emotion. "Please," she repeated, tears burning her eyes. *Please, God. I can't take any more today.*

Just like that, their mother calmed and rested a frail hand on Emory's cheek. "Baby, what's wrong? Why are you crying?"

Emory bit back a sob. "I'm just so happy."

"You were always such a happy child." Her mother patted her cheek, then neared the Christmas tree, lifting the gingerbread man. "Emory, baby, where is that good looking fella you're about to marry? I sure do like him. He brings me the best gingersnaps. Will you tell him I need more? I ate the last one yesterday. It was so delicious."

It always amazed Emory what snippets her mother remembered. Big moments like their father's death escaped her, while small things like cookies that Christian used to bring her stayed in her mind. Emory swiped away a tear. "I'll tell him, Mom."

"Thank you, sweetie." She drew her girls into her arms. "You two take such good care of me."

"Because we love you, Mommy," Jordyn said, whipping away her own trail of tears.

"I love you girls, too." She smiled, but then frowned. "Emory, baby, where is your father? He's supposed to bring me my coffee. He knows exactly how I like it. Four sugars, three creams."

Emory held her tight. "I know he does, Mom. He'll be here any minute."

Chapter 3

It'd been exactly one week since Christian stood face-to-face with Emory, and every day since, he'd seen her face in his dreams. Sleeping and awake. He sat in his SUV and watched her through the oversized window of her shop. *The Bloom Bloom Room*. He chuckled. *Catchy*.

This really could be considered creepy as hell. When he'd left the site where his new office building was being constructed, he'd set a course for home. Somehow he'd ended up here, idling outside the place of business of the woman he'd once believed was his soul mate. What would Emory think if she knew he was stalking her from his vehicle?

He laughed at himself. Stalking was a stretch. *Observing*. Yeah, that sounded better. Regardless of whatever term he used, he shouldn't have been there. Maybe it was everything Chauncey had told him Emory was going through. Maybe it was his guilty conscious gnawing at him. Or maybe he'd just felt the urge to see her one last time, because he damn sure refused to step foot in that shop with Yasmin again.

Yasmin. Wasn't he supposed to miss her? Or at the very least think about her more than he had. Instead of his thoughts lingering on his bride-to-be, they rooted on the one person whom he should have been eager to forget.

The tap on his window startled him. He whipped his head around to see Emory's sister Jordyn grinning in at him. *Shit.* He'd been busted. When he lowered the window, a gust of cold air rushed inside, and an instant chill raced up his spine. Damn, he hated cold weather. "Jordyn? Hey."

A half-smirk, half-smile played at her lips. "I thought that was you. Longtime no see."

"Yeah, it has been a while. I hope you've been well."

"I have, thank you. So, whatcha doing?"

Christian glanced toward the brick building, then back to Jordyn. "I... Uh... I was... I mean, I was about to—"

Jordyn rested her hands on her hips, tilted her head, and narrowed her eyes. "Christian St. Claire, are you spying on my sister?"

He released a boisterous laugh. "Spying?" Another chuckle escaped. "No. I was just about to go inside. Emory's doing the flowers for my upcoming *w*..." He couldn't say the word. Why in the hell couldn't he say the word? "We're working together," he settled on saying.

"On your *wedding*, right?"

Why did she have to put so much emphasis on the word? He nodded. "Yeah."

Jordyn tugged at her gray bomber coat. "Well, come on. I'll walk with you."

Shit. "Um…" Fine mess he'd gotten himself into. He couldn't just leave. That would make him look suspicious. Well, more suspicious than this current situation already looked. "Yeah. Okay. Let me just grab my coat." *Shit*.

After the way he'd acted the last time he'd been there, he was surely the last person Emory wanted to see. He'd just say hello, ask a few generic questions about their order, then leave. Simple as that. He could even say Yasmin sent him. This wouldn't be so bad after all. The statement felt like false bravado.

Two minutes later, they were standing inside Emory's workroom. Bunches of fresh flowers littered nearly every inch of the space. Vases and ribbon were also scattered about. Emory did a double take when her eyes settled on him. Beyond his initial shock, he wasn't sure what to expect next—though he visualized one of the cobalt blue vases slicing through the air and clobbering him in the head.

To his delight, Emory didn't lash out at him, but her scrutinizing eyes questioned his presence. "Hey." That seemed like the most logical thing to say.

"Hey," she supplied in return.

Emory's attention shifted to a grinning Jordyn,

before shifting to him again.

"Are you two hanging out now? BFF's?"

She laughed, but he could sense her discomfort.

Jordyn smirked. "No. I found him...crossing the street to come inside."

Thank you, Jordyn. All he needed was for Emory to know he'd been...*observing* her.

"Oh," said Emory.

"Yasmin sent me," he blurted like a fool. So much for sounding convincing.

"Huh." Emory folded her arms across her chest, her forehead wrinkling in a sign of confusion. "I spoke with your *fiancée* earlier. She didn't mention anything about you stopping by."

If he were standing in front of a mirror, he knew his image would reflect the proverbial deer-in-the-headlights. He shrugged. "I...guess she forgot."

Emory eyed him for a silent second. "Yeah. I guess so."

When her attention slid to Jordyn—who was ping-ponging glances between the two of them—he took the moment to chastise himself for being there.

"You're early," Emory said to Jordyn.

Jordyn glanced at her watch. "You said four, right?"

"No. I said five, Jordyn."

"Shoot. I have a class at five, Em." She turned to Christian. "Christian, I'm sure you wouldn't mind taking my sister home, would you? Her car won't start. I keep telling her to junk the heap."

Christian nonchalantly shrugged one shoulder. "Sure, I—"

"I can take a cab," Emory said, cutting him off.

"That's silly, Emory. You have a ride right here," Jordyn said, resting a hand on Christian's shoulder. "Wow, Christian. You're solid as a rock. Have you been working out? Cop a feel, Emory."

Emory tossed Jordyn a narrow-eyed scowl. Whatever that look represented, it wasn't anything good. For some reason, it humored him.

When Emory's eyes returned to him, he shrugged again. "I really don't mind." Besides, it was the least he could do after how he'd treated her.

"Then it's settled," Jordyn said, moving toward the door. "Welcome back to North Carolina, Christian. I'll call you tonight, Em. Love you both." With that, Jordyn was gone.

"Still the same vivacious, Jordyn," Christian said. When he faced Emory, her arms were pulled even tighter across her chest, and the soft expression she'd flashed moments earlier had morphed into a hard frown. *Uh-oh*.

"What are you doing here, Christian? Because I vaguely remember—no, *distinctively* recall—you telling me to stay away from you. Yet, here you are. In *my* shop. And don't insult my intelligence by saying your *fiancée* sent you."

Why did she keep saying fiancée that way? He thought it in his best interest not to ask. "I...wanted to stop by to say I'm sorry to hear about Ms. Anne." When her brows furrowed, he added, "Chauncey told me." He didn't want her to think he'd been checking up on her or anything. 'Course, she still could think that.

Sadness filled her eyes and her hardness softened.

"Thank you." She rested a hand on the side of her neck. "Look, you don't have to wait around. I'm sure you have better things to do. I'm really okay with catching a cab."

"You've made that clear." He gave a half-smile. "Look, Em... I was out of line the last time we spoke. You deserve to be angry at me."

"The truth doesn't anger me, Christian. You simply spoke what was in your heart." She ambled across the room. "Since you insist on staying, you might as well make yourself useful." She passed him a pair of pruning shears.

Christian stirred at the sharp blades as if she'd asked him to perform surgery with them. "The only thing I know about flowers is how to order them."

She picked up a long-stemmed white rose. "All you have to do is snip right about here."

When she passed the flower to him, their fingers grazed. She snatched away, rubbing her hand as if something toxic had been transferred from his flesh to hers.

"I promise I don't have cooties," he said with a smile.

"Try not to cut your finger off," she said, putting some distance between them.

Something told him she'd take great pleasure in

watching him bleed to death. He eyed the rose. *Cut the stem. Sounds easy enough.*

Emory stood a couple of feet down from him, stripping thorns from another bunch of roses, lavender in color. Every few minutes, she'd tossed a glance in his direction, but turned away when he acknowledged her. The silence was deafening. Unable to take it another second, he said, "When did you get into floral design?"

He figured he had a fifty-fifty chance of her responding. For a moment, he assumed the odds were against him. But she finally answered.

"About a year ago. I helped a friend decorate her wedding. I discovered I loved creating art with flowers. I applied for and received a small business loan." She glanced around the room, a hint of admiration in her eyes. "Here I am."

"Business good?"

She shrugged. "It has its ups and downs."

Christian almost expected her to share her troubles with him, but she didn't. Why would she? The days of her sharing with him were over. To be honest, he missed those days. The days they'd lie in bed for hours discussing any and everything under the sun.

He laughed to himself. Not in a million years would he have imagined being here with Emory, clipping flowers, of all things. And, being cordial to one another. He shot a glance in her direction. When they'd first broken up, he'd done his best to scrub her from his thoughts. Now here they were. At one point in his life, he'd have died for this woman. He wasn't a hundred percent sure he still wouldn't.

"What about you?" Emory said. "What are you doing these days?"

The inquiring surprised him. "Still tinkering with airplanes." But she knew that already.

She smiled. "Figures."

He chuckled at the comment. Some of the tension that'd thickened the air earlier dissipated. Things between them felt not so tense anymore.

"Are you excited about your upcoming wedding?"

Christian paused mid-cut. "I'm sure I will be. Closer to the date."

"It's only a few weeks away. How much closer do you need to get?" Emory stiffened. "I'm sorry. I didn't mean to...be all in your business."

He brushed off her words. "No need to apologize."

Things grew quiet between them again. But the silence didn't linger as it had before.

"Yasmin seems like a wonderful women. How did you two meet?"

So she was capable of saying Yasmin's name, instead of *fiancée*. But what was this, question Christian hour? Well, he guessed he should have been happy she was actually talking at all. "Through friends. We've been dating six months." Since he figured that would be her next question.

"Six—?"

Yep, he'd expected that reaction. It was the reaction most people had.

Dousing the surprise in her tone, she continued,

"*Wow*. You proposed after only six months. Is she pregnant or something?"

She released an unsteady laugh, but he remained stone-faced.

Emory's lips parted, but nothing readily escaped. "Oh," she finally said, then snatched her focus away from him. "Congratulations. You really have a lot to celebrate. When... When is she due?"

"She..." His words trailed off. "*We* loss the baby."

Emory rested her hand on her chest. "Oh, God. Christian, I'm so sorry. I didn't know."

When he met her gaze, an overwhelming amount of sympathy was present in her eyes. "How could you?"

Emory passed him a rose and smiled. "You and Yasmin have the rest of your lives to fill your home with babies."

"Yeah," he said. "I guess you're right."

For the next hour, they worked in perpetual silence that drained him. This wasn't how things worked with him and Emory. When they were together, there'd never been a silent or dull moment between them. But things had changed. They were no longer the couple who'd planned to build a home on a secluded country lot and run around barefoot and naked in the woods. Or the couple who'd planned to drive cross-country in an RV, collecting shot glasses they'd never use because neither drank hard liquor. Or the couple who'd planned to have four perfectly cultured kids—three boys and a girl. Or the couple who'd vowed to spoil their grandkids rotten.

The memories beckoned a glance in her direction. Did she ever recall any of those things? He sure as hell did. More often then he cared to admit. His gaze raked over the pecan skin he'd caressed countless times, mulled over the plump lips he'd kissed a thousand times, ventured to the neck his tongue knew well. When gravity drew his focus to her pert breasts, he lost his train of thought—and control of the shears.

"*Shit*," he said, dropping the metal onto the table.

Emory shot to him. "What happened?"

"I cut myself." He glanced at the crimson color seeping from his wound. "*Uh-oh*." The sight of blood was like his kryptonite. His stomach knotted and his limbs grew weak.

"Don't look," Emory said, obviously remembering his aversion. "Come on." She guided him to a sink scattered with stems and leaves and placed his hand under the stream of cold water. "Stay here. I'll get the first aid kit."

He nodded, the room spinning around him. A minute later, she returned.

"This may sting a little."

Before he could protest—or prepare—she poured the alcohol onto his cut. He sucked air through his clinched teeth. "*Shit*." Why did he get the feeling she enjoyed his discomfort? Maybe it'd been the mastermind smirk she flashed.

While she focused on his injury, he focused on her. What in the hell had happened between them? What'd he done so wrong that would force her to end their relationship? What could—?

"What?"

It wasn't until Emory spoke that he realized he'd been starting at her. He shook his head. "Nothing." Because that's what it had to be between them. Nothing. "How bad is it? Do I need stitches?"

"I think you'll live without them." She wrapped his finger in a bandage. "All done."

Replacing the first-aid kit, she said, "You should really pay more attention when handling razor-sharp objects."

That included her. "I was distracted." Before she got the urge to ask by what, he lifted his middle finger. "Thank you for this."

"Did you just flip me off?"

Christian laughed. Just as he was about to dismiss the accusation, Emory's cell phone rang.

"Excuse me."

The way she smiled when she glanced at her phone screen, Christian assumed it was her lover. But then he remembered Chauncey telling him she wasn't dating anyone. Why had he experienced a sense of relief?

Emory's expression changed and worry spread across her face. "Oh, God. I'm on my way."

"What's wrong?"

"My mother—" Emory slapped her hand over her mouth and tears glistened in her eyes. Allowing her hand to fall, she said, "I have to get to the hospital."

He captured her trembling hand, ignoring the

intense sensation her touch caused. "Let's go."

They wasted no time sprinting from the building.

Chapter 4

Emory hadn't realized she was bouncing her leg until Christian rested his hand on her knee. It was something she did when she was anxious. The phone call she'd received about her mother had her rattled. Blinking tears away, her eyes settled on his touch.

Christian snatched his hand away, as if he'd just realized what he'd done. "Sorry." Clearing his throat, he said, "We'll be there shortly. Don't worry."

Don't worry? How could she not worry?

A short time later, they sprinted through the emergency room entrance of Rex Hospital. Emory hurried toward the help desk. "Anne Chambers," she said, interrupting the two chatting women. "What room is she in?"

"Ms. Emory."

Emory glanced toward the familiar Nigerian accent to see her mother's nurse aide. Rushing to the woman, she said, "Ifede, what happened? Is my mother okay?"

The woman was in tears. "I'm so sorry. I'm so sorry."

The words knotted Emory's stomach as she contemplated the worst. She rested her hands on Ifede's shoulders, attempting to maintain a level of calmness. "It's okay. Just tell me what happened."

Ifede glided a trembling hand across her cheek. "I was fixing her meal. I thought she was still sleeping. I heard a sound. Then a crash. When I went into the room, Ms. Anne was on the floor, the Christmas tree laying on top of her."

"Oh, God," Emory said, a queasy feeling overwhelming her. She placed a shaky hand on her stomach. "Where is she? I need to see her."

"She is in x-ray now. The lady said someone will come for you when she's done. I am so sorry," Ifede repeated.

"It's not your fault." Her words were sincere, but she didn't have the energy to comfort the woman beyond that. Emory cradled herself in her arms, feeling absolutely helpless. A beat later, she wandered away from a chatting Ifede and Christian. Standing in front of a large window, she stared out into the darkness.

Her thoughts raked over everything she had on her plate: her overextended business, her ailing mother, the mountain of bills... Christian. She eyed his reflection in the window, then rolled her eyes away. *Now this*. The weight of it all broke her down, and she began to sob.

Without prompting, Christian was at her side,

wrapping her shaking body in his arms. She didn't fight or deny his embrace. Instead, she clung to him. Being in his warm arms was the most peace she'd experienced in months, maybe even years. His arms had always been her serenity, her safe haven. Clearly, that hadn't changed because for a brief moment, the voices of defeat silenced.

"It's okay, Em." A reassuring hand glided up and down her back in a slow, deliberate manner. "It's okay."

Why did his soothing tone still have the ability to calm her frayed nerves? Being in his arms felt so right, but deep down she knew being there was wrong. Him holding her, him comforting her... All wrong. Sure, she could say they were friends, and he was only doing what friends did for one another. But it would be a lie.

They weren't friends. They were ex-lovers. Ex-lovers who'd once shared a connection so deep they could have been one body. Ex-lovers who'd planned a beautiful life together. Ex-lovers who'd not gotten their happily ever after. Ex-lovers who shouldn't be entangled in each other's arms.

"The doctor's here," Christian said in a tender tone.

Emory pulled away from Christian's chest, their gazes locking briefly. What she saw set her soul on fire. Denying the burn, she forced her gaze away before she was consumed by Christian's scorching flame. "How is my mother?"

The doctor—a tall, thin man with auburn hair and a face full of freckles—flashed a warm smile. "Just fine.

Luckily, there are no broken bones or internal injuries. She's a little battered and bruised, but otherwise okay."

Emory cupped her hands under her chin. "Thank God." Christian stood beside her, giving her a reassuring squeeze on the shoulder. His touch rippled through her like an electric current.

"We've placed her in a room. We're going to keep her overnight," Dr. Ripley—as his nametag read— continued, "Just for observation."

"Of course," Emory said. "Can I see her, doctor?"

"Absolutely. Keep in mind, we've given her something to calm her down. She was a bit...*rambunctious* when they tried to do the x-ray. We see that frequently in Alzheimer's patients."

God, she hated that word. When her mother had been diagnosed with middle-stage Alzheimer's two years ago, Emory's life came to a screeching halt. Her mother became her number one priority. Which meant everything else took a backseat.

Turning to Christian, she said, "Thank you for everything."

"Do you mind if I come with you?" he asked.

Emory stilled a moment, the question taking her by surprise. "Ah, sure." Though she doubted her mother would recognize him.

When they entered the room, her mother lay flat on the mattress wringing her hands and staring at the ceiling. Emory approached the bed cautiously, not wanting to startle her. "Mom?" she said in a whisper.

Her mother's face lit up. "Emory, baby? Is that

you?"

"Yes, it's me." She took her mother's outreached hand. "How do you feel?"

Her mother frowned. "I'm so tired."

"I know. The doctor said they gave you something that will help you rest. You sleep. I'm right here."

Ms. Anne's gaze slid past her. "Who's with you?"

"Hello, Ms. Anne," Christian said, moving closer.

Ms. Anne's eyes brightened. "Christian St. Claire?"

Emory's head snapped back in surprise. It'd been so long since she'd seen him. She took it as a good sign that her mother recognized him.

Christian donned a confident smile. "Yes, ma'am."

"Oh, come here, son, and give me a hug."

Christian bent and her mother wrapped him in her frail arms. Emory loved days like this. When her mother remembered the small things. When she wasn't forgetting the address of the house she'd lived in for forty-five years, or her phone number, or the fact that her husband had died. Emory loved when there weren't mood swings or empty stares out the window. Loved when there was no confusion about what year it was.

On the days Anne Madell Chambers—ex-school teacher, ballroom dancing instructor, songbird— surfaced, Emory rejoiced.

"It's so good to see you, son," Ms. Anne said. "I'm so glad you two are back together. I prayed about it. God don't make no mistakes."

"Mom, we're—"

"I prayed about it, too, Ms. Anne," Christian said.

Emory nearly choked on her own tongue. When Christian tossed her a glance, she understood why he'd said what he'd said. He simply wanted her mother to experience some form of happiness. She swallowed any protest she may have had about the statement. Tomorrow, her mother wouldn't even remember the conversation.

Emory eased into one of the chairs near her mother's bed. A short time later, Jordyn arrived. Christian and Jordyn kept Ms. Anne entertained, while Emory vanished into her own thoughts. It was like old times, the four of them sitting around chatting and laughing. For a moment, things actually felt normal in her life.

When Emory checked her watch, it was close the nine o'clock. Where had the time gone? "Mom, we have to go now, but I'll be back first thing in the morning. You'll get to go home." The fact that Jordyn had volunteered to stay the night with their mother eased Emory's reservations about leaving.

Ms. Anne laughed. "Sweetie, what are you talking about? I am home." She searched the room. "I…think." Her brow furrowed. "Where am I?"

And just like that, her mother had been snatched away again.

"You're in the hospital, Mommy," Jordyn said. "I'm going to stay the night with you."

Her mother smiled brightly. "Okay. You girls are so good to me."

Emory bent and kissed her mother's forehead. "I

love you, songbird," she said.

"I love you, too, sweetie."

Christian squeezed Ms. Anne's hand. "I'll see you soon, Ms. Anne,"

Ms. Anne took Christian's hand into hers, a somber expression spreading over her face. "Please forgive me."

Jordyn tossed Emory a questioning glance and Emory shrugged. For all Emory knew, her mother could have thought Christian was a priest to whom she could confess her sins. Emory feared what would come out of her mouth.

Christian smiled down at Ms. Anne. "Forgive you for what?"

"For being the reason my daughter broke your heart." She snuggled under the covers and closed her eyes.

Christian and Jordyn tossed questioning glances in her directions. If she had to guess, they both wondered the same thing: whether or not the statement was true. Emory shrugged, suggesting she had no idea what her mother was talking about and hoped to end it there. Unfortunately, by the look in Christian's eyes, she knew it wouldn't be that simple.

Chapter 5

Christian tried to force Ms. Anne's words out of his head. But they lingered—torturing and teasing him. What did she mean by being the reason Emory had broken his heart? Could that truly have been the reason Emory ended their relationship? *Nah*.

The idea was ridiculous, right? Emory had known him better than that. Had to have known he would have stood by her side. He tossed a quick glance at his passenger. If he asked her, would she tell him the truth? Did he want to know the truth? Could he handle the truth?

No way was her mother's condition the reason she'd walked away. Again, he attempted to force the thought away. Had to force it away, before it drove him insane.

Emory's stomach growled. They'd been at the hospital for hours. The only thing either of them had consumed was a cup of lukewarm coffee. "Are you hungry?" As if he really needed to ask.

"No." Her stomach protested the answer. "Maybe a little."

"So am I. Let's get something to eat."

"I… I don't think that's a good idea."

"Why?"

Emory shifted toward him. "What would your *fiancée* say about you having dinner with your…florist?"

"I'm not having dinner with a florist. I'm having dinner with an old friend."

"*Old friend*?"

"Yes," he said, cautiously. Though, by the emphasis she'd placed on the word, he had a feeling he'd regret using the label.

"Does your fiancée know you and your *old friend* used to be lovers?"

Yep, he'd walked right into that one. No, he hadn't told Yasmin about their history because, at the time, he hadn't seen the need. And truthfully, he didn't see one now. What would it accomplish? Other than making it an even more awkward situation than it already was. Plus, he was pretty sure Yasmin would fire Emory on the spot. He wouldn't allow that to happen. Emory needed the business.

Christian redirected his attention in front of him without answering her.

Emory chuckled. "I didn't think so."

She straightened in her seat and returned her focus outside the window, fingering the pendant dangling from her necklace.

Approaching a red light, Christian said, "You still wear it."

"What?" Emory asked, clearly lost in her own thoughts.

"The angel wings. You still wear them."

She dipped her head and eyed the diamond encrusted piece he'd given her. Tucking it beneath the sweater she wore, she said, "Got to stay protected, right?"

"Is that the only reason?" *Damn*. Where had that come from? And how'd he allow the reckless words to escape?

"What other reason would there be?"

He could think of a few, but none of them really mattered. They eyed each other for a long moment that bordered uncomfortable. For the first time since he could recall, something terrified him. That something... the feelings reconnecting with Emory brought to the surface and his inability to deny them.

"The light is green," she said.

"What?"

Before she could repeat herself, a car horn blared behind them.

She tossed a glance over her shoulder. "You better go before there's a case of road rage. You know how grumpy people get at Christmas."

He pulled off. "Everyone except you. I don't think I've ever known anyone who loves Christmas as much as you do."

"Yeah. I used to. The last few years…" She sighed heavily. "Christmas just doesn't feel the same. I can't seem to get into the holiday spirit."

With everything she had going on, how could she possibly be in a festive mood? But he asked anyway, "Any particular reason?"

She eyed her fidgeting fingers. "There's just a lot going on in my life. I don't really want to go into detail."

He nodded, respecting her decision, but wished she'd talk to him like old times. Then it hit him. These weren't old times. These were new times. And in these new times, he was no longer the shelter she ran to when she needed refuge from the storm.

A short time later, they pulled in front of Emory's ranch-style home. Something inside of him hated their time together had come to an end. The same something that told him he knew he had to see her again. Another something reminded him of the fact that he was weeks from getting married, which meant whatever this was drawing him to Emory had to be contained. This had to be the last time he saw her. He had no other choice.

"Thank you so much, Christian, for altering your day for me. You didn't have to, but I'm grateful you did."

"What are friends for?"

Unfastening her seatbelt, she said, "Yeah, what are friends for?"

Why had her words sounded so condescending? Did she believe he was trying to be patronizing? "I'll walk you to the door," he said.

"That's not necessary. Besides, it's freezing out. You hate cold weather. Or, at least, you used to."

He still did, but he wasn't sure even the forty degree temperature outside could penetrate the heat raging inside of him. The kind of heat he should feel for the woman he was about to marry, but never had. The kind of heat that reminded him when you play with fire, you get burned.

"Have a good night, Christian." She smiled and closed the door.

He watched as she strolled toward the house, growing more and more anxious with each step she took away from him. *Don't do it, Christian. Don't do it*, his inner voice warned. Lowering the window, he called out. "What time should I pick you up in the A.M.?"

Emory stopped but didn't readily face him. When she finally did, he swore moonlight glistened off of her cheeks. Had she been crying?

"You don't have to do that, Christian. Jordyn can pick me up."

"Jordyn has class in the morning." When she flashed him a questioning expression, he added, "She told me when you stepped out of the room."

He couldn't decipher whether or not she bought his fib. But if she called to verify it with Jordyn, he would be in a pickle.

"I can get Lucas to pick me up."

Who the hell was Lucas? Then he remembered the man with the Australian accent that'd showed him into the conference room. Dismissing her option, he said,

"What time, Emory?"

She folded her arms across her chest. "Don't you have a job you should be reporting to?"

"Not for another month or so. Six o'clock... Seven o'clock?"

She nestled her coat tighter, glanced up and down the street as if she were trying to ascertain whether or not anyone was watching, then sighed heavily. "Nine."

"Nine o'clock it is."

"*Goodnight*, Christian." She turned, jogged to the house and disappeared inside.

"Goodnight, Emory," he mumbled to himself.

He'd masked his motives behind a thick cloak of "just being a friend," but this was far more than being there for a friend in need. This was dangerous. Yet, he continuously chose to ignore the risks.

Had he forgotten that this was the woman who'd shattered his hearts? Damn. He really needed to get his head straight.

Need.

Was that it? Did he *need* to be near her? He tossed a glance at the closed door. The question troubled him. Mainly because he knew with Emory was the last place he *needed* to be.

***

The following morning, Christian arrived at Emory's place a half hour early. He refused to admit— even to himself—that the reason he'd been so punctual was because he couldn't wait to see her again. Instead, he contributed it to the fact that, like Emory, he favored punctuality.

As he stepped onto the porch, Charles Brown's "Please Come Home for Christmas," greeted his ears. He rang the bell and waited. The music lowered and light footsteps grew closer and closer. When Emory eased the door open, she was still in her night clothes— a pair of hot pink flannel pajama pants imprinted with tiny snowflakes, and a white tank top that appeared a size too small. Despite her tousled hair and weary expression, she was still gorgeous.

"Good morning," he said, focusing on her eyes and not her nipples—that beaded from the rush of cold air. At least, that's what he assumed it was from. What else could it have been?

"You're early."

"Am I?" He flipped his wrist to glance at his watch. "Huh. I guess I am." Pointing over his shoulder, he said, "I can wait in the vehicle." For a moment, he thought she'd agree with him.

"Don't be ridiculous. It's like two degrees out there."

He shivered for effect. "Yeah, it is pretty cold out *here*." He hoped his emphasis on *here* would prompt her to invite him inside.

She stepped aside. "Come in."

When he ambled through the threshold, the first thing to hit him was the scent of cinnamon. He searched for the rustic broom he knew was the culprit. It lay on the marble in front of a crackling fireplace.

The room had changed. The red leather sectional had been replaced with two brown sofas that reclined on either end. Abstract art graced the walls. Noting the initials in the bottom right-hand corner, he said. "Did you—"

Emory's taut nipples appeared more pronounced, causing him to lose his train of thought. Fighting his way out of the stupor and finding her eyes again, he said, "Ahm... Did you paint these?"

Emory claimed a sweater draped over the arm of a chair and slid into it. He felt like an asshole—more like a pervert—for ogling her breasts. *So much for being a gentleman*. Luckily, she didn't call him out on the action.

"Yes, I painted them."

"Wow. Nice."

"Thank you."

"You're just full of all kind of creative surprises."

"Flowers and painting are outlets for me."

He nodded with understanding.

She pointed over her shoulder. "It'll only take me a minute to shower and dress."

"Take your time," he said, scrutinizing every inch of the room.

"There's hot chocolate on the stove. Help yourself. There are marshmallows, too." She flashed a knowing smile.

"Homemade hot chocolate? I see you still know how to please me." He stilled. *Damn*. He hadn't meant it like it'd come out. "I wasn't suggesting you made it just for me or anything. What I meant—"

Emory lifted her hand. "Actually, I did make it just for you. My way of saying thank you. Again."

Before he could respond, his cell phone sounded.

Emory backed away. "I'll let you take that. I'll be out shortly."

He nodded and fished his cell phone from his pocket as Emory disappeared down the hall. His grandmother's name flashed across the screen. *This should be interesting.*

Chapter 6

Emory found herself in the same dire situation she'd been in the day before. Fighting her lingering attraction to Christian. Why hadn't she gone with her first instinct and called a cab before he arrived to chauffeur her to work?

Because you're an idiot, that's why. What in the hell are you doing here, Emory? You know better than this. You're not a homewrecker. But was she truly committing a crime? She glanced over at Christian behind the steering wheel. *Yes*. One of deep passion.

Emory released an inward groan. This man grew more and more handsome by the second. To think, all of him used to be hers. Those soft lips could once tame her with just a brush across hers. Broad shoulders that'd once carried the weight of any of her worries on them. Powerful arms that'd held her when she'd needed to be comforted—or just held close to him. Arms she needed wrapped around her now, ensuring her that everything would be fine.

"Everything okay?" he asked.

Jolting from the fact she'd been caught staring at him, she nodded and turned away from his prying eyes. *Let him go, Emory*. The command was as hard to follow now as it had been two years ago. Spending time with him only made it more difficult to comprehend the fact that he belonged to someone else. His presence reminded her of how good they were together. Reminded her of just how much she'd missed this man in her life.

As routine, she repeated to herself that she'd sacrificed her happiness for Christian's. That knowledge did little to fill the empty hole in her heart losing him had created.

The words his grandmother spat at her like venom the night before Emory ended things with Christian played in her head. Recalling the woman's harsh, cruel tone made Emory feel like that weak and broken girl who'd stood in the foyer of the St. Claire manor and lied to the man she loved. Why had she been so weak?

"Daydreaming?"

Christian's words grounded her in present time. "Just listening to the song. It's one of my favorites." Of course, she really hadn't needed to tell him that.

With the press of a finger, he increased the volume and Mariah Carey's "All I Want for Christmas is You," filled the cabin. He winked, then returned his focus to the road ahead.

Emory didn't seem to be the only one with a lot on their mind. Christian hadn't said much since they'd left her place. Something was obviously troubling him. Did it have something to do with the phone call he'd taken? Had it been Yasmin on the opposite end? If so, did hearing her voice cause him guilt for being there with Emory?

Emory lowered the volume and Mariah's voice faded. "Are you okay, Christian? You seem preoccupied."

He nodded slowly. "I'm good."

The weak smile he flashed wasn't overly convincing, but who was she to dispute. If he said he was good, he was good. "Okay." Her focus shifted back out the window, but it didn't stay there long. "It's just that you seem like something is troubling you."

Christian flashed a half-smile. "That's cute."

"What's cute?"

"Your concern."

Emory rolled her eyes away. "Whatever. Just can't be nice to some people without them taking it out of context." Facing him again, she said, "And for the record, I'm not concerned. I just wanted to make sure you were focused on driving. I don't want you to run me into a telephone pole or something."

He barked a laugh. "Well, gee, thanks for your *non* concern. I'll do my very best to keep you alive. I wouldn't want your death on my conscious."

"Good."

"Fine."

She reached forward and cranked the volume on the radio. "Fantastic."

Coming to a red light, he shut the radio off. "Do you always have to get the last word?"

She was about to say something snarky and clever, but the way Christian's eyes raked over her face muted her. His eyes lowered to her parted lips—lingering way too long for comfort, in her opinion. The temperature inside the SUV tripled. This man was turning her into a fool for love.

Banishing the quiver in her stomach, the pressure between her thighs, and the hum in her heart, she said, "Light's green," in a low, yielding tone that she hadn't meant to use.

"So it is," he said, the road ahead reclaiming his attention.

Christian pulled away from the light and made a right onto Person Street, forcing Emory to bolt forward in the seat. "Ah, where are we going? My shop—and car—are both in the opposite direction."

"Breakfast. I'm starving."

Was he serious? Hadn't they already established that dining together was not a good idea? Did he believe that had changed? "I really need to have my car running this morning, Christian. I have to pick my mother up from the hospital. You can't continue to chauffeur me around town. I've occupied too much of your time already." *And you've consumed far too many of my thoughts*.

"Did I not mention I had your car towed first thing

this morning? One of my boys owns an auto body shop off of New Bern Avenue."

Had my car towed first thing this morning?

"He originally thought it was the battery, but discovered acid had leaked and corroded some wires. There were a few other issues, too. *Major* issues. When was the last time you had that vehicle serviced?"

She hadn't. Anything other than the standard oil change required additional monies. Funds she didn't have. Had her car towed? A vision of an astronomical bill played in her head. Lifting his phone from the center console, she pushed it toward him and said, "You should call him before he gets started."

Christian's brow furrowed. "Call him for what?"

"*Because—*" She closed her eyes briefly to steady her tone. Meeting his questioning gaze, she sighed a sound of defeat. "Because I can't afford it, Christian." Her pride took a hit, but she'd always been able to be honest with Christian without judgement.

"But I can. It's already taken care of, Emory. It won't cost you anything. Other than a few more hours with me. But if that's so unbearable, I can rent you a car."

"I don't need you to take care of it, Christian. I don't need you to take care of *me*. Call him." She wasn't good at playing the damsel in distress.

"No. You're being ridiculous, Em."

Emory shifted in her seat. "Call him."

Christian laughed, but it lacked humor. "You're still as stubborn as hell. Will you please swallow some of that pride and let me help you?"

"And you want what in return?"

Apparently, her words struck a sour note with Christian, because he veered the SUV off the shoulder so fast, she nearly suffered whiplash.

Facing her with furrowed brows, he said, "I don't want anything in return. Is that why you think I'm doing this? Because I want something from you?"

"I don't know what to think. Why *are* you doing it? Why are you being so kind to me? Just a week ago you were ready to strangle me in my conference room. Why the change?"

His jaw flexed, then relaxed. The fight she saw in his eyes fizzled, and the tension present in his shoulders relaxed.

"We loved each other once, Emory. You're going through something. I just want to help. That's all. Nothing more, nothing less."

They stared at each other for a long, hard moment. If she'd wanted to say more, she wouldn't have been able to. Not after what he'd just said. After what felt like an eternity connected to him, she turned away and settled against the seat.

A beat later, he pulled back into traffic.

"Thank you," she mumbled. "I'll pay you back every cent."

"And I won't accept it."

Emory folded her arms across her chest and rode that way until Christian pulled into the parking lot of her favorite breakfast spot. A place she hadn't visited since they'd split. *Why here of all places*?

Christian pulled into a space alongside the Citi Café, popped the gear shift into park, killed the engine, and opened his door. "Are we going to have breakfast, or are you going to just sit there and pout?"

Oh, he played dirty. He knew she couldn't resist. Giving him the evil eye, she said, "Well, if I have to put up with you, I guess I shouldn't have to do it on an empty stomach."

He released a hearty laugh, then shook his head. "You don't spare a punch, do you?"

Before he could get around to her side of the vehicle, Emory was out and moving toward the restaurant. Jesus, her legs hurt. Why had she chosen last night to go overboard with the squats? She tossed a glance over her shoulder at Christian. He was why. She'd needed some way to quiet the sexual frustration he'd caused.

Christian reached around her to open the door, but she plowed through before he could. Admittedly, she was being a brat to the one person going out of his way to help her. It wasn't that she didn't appreciate his efforts, because she most certainly did. It was that his kindness reminded her of why she'd fallen in love with him in the first place. That big heart of his. She didn't need any more reminders that she still loved him, dammit.

The second they were inside, someone called out to them. When Emory rotated in the direction of her name, Passion Phillips, Citi's proprietor, waddled across

66

the room toward them. The woman was as pregnant as pregnant could get.

"Oh, my God. It's like seeing two ghosts." Passion hugged Emory, then Christian.

"You look amazing, Passion," Emory said. "You definitely have a motherly glow."

Passion rested hand against her forehead. "I look—and feel—like I'm about to explode, but thank you for the compliment."

"How far along are you?" Emory asked.

"Six months."

Christian's eyes widened. "Six months? Are you having twins?"

Emory swatted him playfully.

"It's okay," Passion said with a laugh. "Everyone has the same reaction. No. There's only one in the oven."

Emory couldn't believe Passion still had three more months to go. The woman looked over baked.

Passion rested her hands on her hips. "Where have you two been?"

Emory dreaded the question. How did she answer it? She looked to Christian for guidance, but he simply folded his arms across his chest and rocked back and forth on his heels as if he couldn't wait to hear her response.

Luckily, before Emory was forced to craft some plausible tale, Passion was summoned to the kitchen. Emory blew out a sigh of relief.

"Sit anywhere you'd like," Passion said, wobbling

away.

"Saved by the bell," Christian said under his breath.

She elbowed him in the ribs.

Sliding into one of the booths near the back of the restaurant, Emory immediately lowered her eyes to the menu. "I'm starving." She could feel Christian's gaze settled on her, but she refused to look up at him. He did that a lot, she'd noted, watched her as if he were trying to decode her thoughts.

Cautiously meeting his gaze, a hint of nervousness rippled through her. What did he see when he eyed her? Maybe he saw the woman who'd promised to always love him. Maybe he saw the woman who'd promised to always be his. Maybe he saw the woman who'd promised him a house full of babies. "*Girls as gorgeous as their mother,*" he'd said. "*And boys as handsome as their father,*" she'd said in return.

Maybe he didn't see any of that. Maybe he saw the woman who'd lied about it all. *Except about loving him forever*, she told herself. That promise she'd kept. Too bad he would never know it.

"I have to ask you something, Emory. It's been eating at me. I know it shouldn't because it doesn't matter, but…"

Uh-oh. Whatever it was, she was sure she wasn't ready for it. "Okay."

Christian rested his elbows on the table, intertwined his fingers, and eyed them briefly. Glancing up at her, he said, "What your mother said about her being the reason you…" He stopped briefly. "That wasn't—"

Her reply was swift. "No." Unable to get a read on his facial expression, Emory wasn't sure if he believed her or not.

Finally, he interrupted the awkwardness.

"So, you'd really just fallen out of love with me?"

And made it that much more uncomfortable.

"Shit. Forget I said that," Christian said. "We were a long time ago. What's the use of dwelling on the past? We've both moved on, right?"

You've moved on, she wanted to say. "Yes, we have. Just think, you'll be married soon. Not many people are so lucky to find their soul mate after only six months of dating. You should consider yourself blessed." God, did she sound bitter? Yes. Lowering her eyes to the menu again, she said, "Their soup of the day is She-Crab. I remember the first time I ever had She-Crab soup. We were—"

She stopped abruptly, the smile the memory had elicited sliding from her face. The first time she'd had the soup was on a trip they'd taken to Kiawah Island in South Carolina. It'd also been the first time they'd made love. The weekend had been so beautiful, so perfect that it could have been mistaken for a dream. But it hadn't been a dream. She'd pinched herself numerous times to make sure.

"Our trip to Kiawah Island," he said.

Emory massaged the side of her neck. "Yeah."

"That was a good weekend. *Great* weekend,

actually."

A cautious smile lifted the corners of her mouth. "Yeah, it was. Well, except for me running over a rock and crashing into the bushes."

Christian chuckled. "You scared the hell out of me that day. I just knew you'd seriously injured yourself."

"The only thing I injured was my pride. And elbow." She lifted her arm. "My battlefield wound."

She hadn't expected Christian to reach across the table and glide his index finger across her scar. The sensation made her tingle all over. Withdrawing her arm, she said, "You took good care of me."

He shrugged. "That's what you do when you love someone."

The words made her heart thump a little harder, her breathing a little more swallow. Unable to maintain their eye contact a second longer, she lowered her eyes back to the menu. "Every..." The words stuck in her throat. Clearing it, she said, "Everything sounds so delicious."

"Do you ever think about us, Emory? About what could have been?"

She closed her eyes. Why would he put her against the wall like this? Did she lie and say no? Did she tell the truth and say every single day of her life? Her heart made the decision for her. Meeting his gaze, she exhaled a slow, steady breath. "Of course I do. You were my best friend."

Christian's jaw flexed, and she wondered what words he bit back. As if he'd never posed the question, his eyes left her. But a blink later, they settled on her again.

There, in his penetrating stare, the questions lingered. She hadn't done a grand job of answering them back then, and she doubted she'd do much better now. Before any words could escape past his lips, she intervened. "Don't, Christian. Please."

Their gazes held a long time, each passing second reminding her she'd made a mistake two years ago. She'd made the wrong decision for what she thought were the right reasons. Now it was too late to make things right.

As crazy as it seemed, she couldn't shake the feeling that he still felt something for her. Of course, the voice in her head worked to debunk the thought with its own unsolicited commentary:

Why are you deluding yourself? He's getting married. Married! M-A-R-R-I-E-D. The only woman he has feelings for is his fiancée. Fiancée! F-I-A-N-C-É-E."

Cleary, the voice in her head thought she was not only delusional, but illiterate, too. Though harsh in its approach, she couldn't dismiss it. Maybe she was delusional to think that after what she'd done to him Christian could still love her.

Chapter 7

By the time Christian and Emory arrived at the hospital, it was a little after twelve. They'd swung by the auto body shop to get some things Emory needed from her vehicle. It would be at least another three days before her car was ready.

The second they walked into Ms. Anne's room, Christian knew he was in trouble.

"Jordyn? What are you doing here?" Emory asked.

Jordyn flashed a quizzical expression. "I spent the night, remember?" She smirked and crossed her arms over her chest. "Christian, what did you do to my sister to make her suffer memory loss?"

Emory shot Jordyn a scowl that could have leveled a mountain. He was smart enough not to entertain the question. Instead, he flashed his palms. Before long, he was sure he'd be dealing with his own form of Emory-wrath. Especially when she discovered he'd lied about

Jordyn going to class.

"Did you not go to class? You know I don't like you skipping class?"

Jordyn's brow arched. "Class? I didn't have class today. Why'd you think I had class?"

When Emory slid a narrow-eyed gaze in his direction, Christian flashed a half-smile.

"You said my sister asked you to pick me up because she had class."

He'd had a feeling that lie would come back to bite him in the ass.

Jordyn snapped her fingers and popped her forehead. "You know what? Yes, I did tell Christian that. It totally slipped my mind. The class was cancelled. Last minute. You know how that goes."

Emory tossed suspicious glances at them both, but didn't call either of them out. Instead, she shook her head and neared her mother sitting on the side of the bed and wrapped the woman into a warm embrace.

When Emory excused herself to assist their mother into the bathroom, he turned to Jordyn. "Thank you."

"You're welcome. But you know she didn't buy that, right?"

Oh, he knew. "I'm sure she'll let me know that later."

"I've been meaning to ask you something, Christian."

Why did he get the feeling he wouldn't like whatever it was? "Sure. Anything." He regretted the anything part the second it slipped out.

Jordyn tilted her head to one side. "How does that work, exactly?"

Confused, he said, "How does what work?"

"How do you marry another woman when it's painfully obvious you're still in love with my sister?"

The statement took him by surprise and Jordyn must have seen it on his face.

"Tough question, huh?" She tossed a glance toward the bathroom door, obviously to make sure Emory was still on the opposite side of it. "I love my sister, Christian, and I don't want to see her hurt."

"I would never hurt Emory, Jordyn. You know that." Despite how much she'd hurt him.

"I know you wouldn't intentionally hurt her. But what do you think is going to happen when you and your *wife* ride off into the sunset?"

This time, Christian glanced at the closed bathroom door.

"She still loves you, Christian. And I know you still love her. But you have to walk away."

The bathroom door cracked open and Emory and their mother exited. The smile on Emory's face faded away. Had she sensed the tension in the room?

"What's going on?" Emory asked.

"Nothing," Jordyn said, playfully. "Just catching up with Christian."

Christian slid his hands in his pockets and flashed a forced smile.

Any future inquiry Emory intended was thwarted

by the entry of their mother's doctor. Christian watched the man's lips move, but he hadn't heard a single word. Jordyn's words bounced around inside his head like a ping-pong ball. As much as he hated to admit it, she'd been right. He needed to walk away. But how?

"Christian?"

Emory's voice penetrated his thoughts. "I'm sorry. What did you say?"

"Do you mind playing chauffeur once more? I think it'll be easier for mom to get in and out of your SUV than Jordyn's Hyundai."

"Absolutely," he said.

"Thank you."

She eyed him a second, as if trying to read his mind. Oh, she definitely didn't want to be in his head now. His tangled thoughts would frighten her. Hell, they even alarmed him.

By the time Ms. Anne was actually discharged, it was close to four in the afternoon. Christian had made plans to have dinner with his grandmother at six. He still had plenty of time to get home, shower, and make it to the manor with time to spare.

"Earth to Christian," Emory said. When he faced her, she laughed. "What's going on with you? At the hospital. Now. You keep zoning out."

Ms. Anne chimed in from the backseat, sparing him from having to answer Emory.

"Handsome fella. Can we get doughnuts?"

Christian eyed Ms. Anne through the rearview mirror. "Pretty lady, you can have whatever you want."

Ms. Anne grinned like she'd just been crowned prom queen.

Emory eyed him as if he'd committed a crime. "What?"

She glanced over her shoulder at her mother, then back to him. In a muted tone, she said, "My mother is like a boisterous five-year-old when she gets sugar. Jordyn and I will be chasing her around the house all night."

"Raspberry," her mother yelled.

They both laughed.

When they settled, Emory eyed him again. God, she was beautiful. "What did I do this time?"

She shook her head. "Nothing."

Her focus shifted through the windshield, but moments later drifted to him again.

"Come on. What?" he asked with a hint of laughter in his tone.

"Thank you. I won't forget everything you've done for me."

"And a vanilla milkshake," Ms. Anne blurted.

Christian smirked, then eyed Ms. Anne through the mirror again. "Anything you—"

Emory jabbed a finger at him. "*Shush*."

He grabbed her hand and pretended to bite her finger. The feel of her flesh against his caused a tingle inside his palm. After what he'd experienced in the hospital lobby when he'd held her shaking body in his arms, he'd vowed to keep his hands to himself. She clouded his already foggy judgment.

Emory chuckled. "Pay attention to the road. You're carrying precious cargo."

"Yes ma'am."

"No one's holding my hand," Ms. Anne said.

Christian and Emory exchanged confused glances.

"Mom, what are you—?"

Emory's eyes lowered and his followed. Their hands were locked in an intimate hold. Emory cautiously pulled away from him. He rested his hand in his lap and made a fist to preserve the lingering sensation.

How in the hell had that happened? Him holding her hand and neither realizing it. It didn't take him long to craft the explanation: their connection had always been so natural.

The rest of their trip was made in silence. When they pulled into Ms. Anne's driveway, he stared at the two-story powder blue house. It brought back a lot of memories. Some of the best moments of his life had been made inside that love-filled house.

Ms. Anne opened her door and slid out. She didn't protest the fact they hadn't stopped for doughnuts and milkshakes. He just assumed she'd forgotten she'd asked for the things. If only he could forget his feelings for Emory with such ease.

"I'll help you get your mother inside," he said, unbuckling his seatbelt. He half expected Emory to play her usual superwoman role and protest his assistance, but she didn't.

"Okay. You ready, Mom?"

The way Emory cared for her mother filled him with a great deal of respect for her—even more than he already harbored. She was so endearing and loving toward the woman. She hadn't lost her nurturing manner.

Ms. Anne swatted Emory away, then clung to his arm. "I want handsome to help me."

"I got it," he said.

"Yeah, he's got it," said Ms. Anne.

Emory flashed her palms. "Fine."

When they opened the door, they were greeted by the toppled Christmas tree. Icy blue bulbs—some whole, others shattered—littered the hardwood. A black Santa topper rested near a worn dark gray recliner.

"Oh, dear." Ms. Anne said, resting her thin hand on her chest. "What a mess."

"Don't worry about this, gorgeous. I'll make it just like new," Christian said.

Ms. Anne beamed. "You're such a good man. You remind me of my husband." With a delicate touch, she patted his cheek. "I'm glad you asked for my daughter's hand. I'm proud to call you my son." Ms. Anne released her hold on him. "Can we play some Christmas music?"

A nervous smile slid across Emory's face. "I'm sorry about that. With this disease, she can see something on television and believe it actually happened. The other day she asked if she could go with me alligator hunting. She'd been watching *Swamp People*."

"I understand," he said, but knew Ms. Anne wasn't

recalling some random moment she'd seen on TV. The day before Emory had ended their relationship, he had asked her mother for her hand. He'd just never got the opportunity to propose. "Don't sweat it."

Ms. Anne cranked the radio. Chuck Berry's "Run, Run Rudolph" blasted through the speakers.

Emory yelled over the deafening music as she crossed the room. "Mom, maybe we should turn it down a little. We don't want the neighbors to call the police on us for disturbing the peace."

"I guess you're right," Ms. Anne said. "I think I'd like to take a nap, dear."

"Okay." Emory excused them and disappeared down the hall.

Christian started the task of erecting the Christmas tree. It was a bit unstable, and he was concerned it would topple over again. Tomorrow, he could— He abandoned the thought. There would be no tomorrow. He needed to distance himself from Emory. It was for the best. He'd have a rental car delivered so she wouldn't have to work around Jordyn's schedule. That's the least he could do.

He was partially responsible for why she didn't have her car, but he didn't regret having it towed. That hunk of metal had been on its last leg. He'd purchase her a new car, if he thought there was any fraction of a chance she'd accept it.

By the time Emory returned, he'd almost finished with the cleanup.

"Christian, you didn't have to do this. I could—"

Without warning or thought, he snatched Emory into his arms. "Watch out."

As suspected, the tree did a nosedive, barely missing her.

Emory stared up at him with tender eyes. Her gaze trailed to his mouth, but only lingered there a short time. "That...was close," she said in an unsteady tone.

"Yeah, it was." Too close. Kinda like they were now.

Emory's hands rested against his chest, his arms around her waist. If there were ever a time he needed strength, it was now. Staring into her inquisitive eyes took him back to the first time they'd met. He recalled the bold statement he'd made to her that day, both soaking wet under a massive oak tree: "*You're going to be my wife.*" He'd only known her an hour, but he just knew.

Christian followed Emory's gaze to the mistletoe that dangled above their heads. Who was he to argue with tradition? "Have you ever been tempted to do something you knew was wrong? Dead wrong. But the temptation to do it outweighed all of the potential risks and outcomes."

"Yes." Her eyes slipped to his mouth again. "Oh,yeah."

"What did you do about it?"

"Nothing. I knew if the decision of whether or not to do it tortured me, then it wasn't something I should do."

Emory closed her eyes as he dragged the pad of

his thumb across her bottom lip. "Sometimes...doing nothing is easier said than done. Sometimes...it's not even an option."

Little mattered in those seconds. Not their derailed past. Not his impending wedding. And certainly not his fiancée. With commonsense neglected, Christian lowered his mouth as close to Emory's as he could get without actually kissing her. Their warm breaths swirled, mixed into a sweet elixir that proved powerful enough to paralyze.

The moment was so intense, so heavily charged with desire that his head spun. His body reacted in the manner any man's body would react when he wanted a woman more than he wanted his next breath. His hardness strained against his zipper, his heart punched against his chest.

No woman had ever made him want more out of life than the woman before him. She'd made him want more, made him do more, made him understand what being a man—a good man—was all about. That particular lesson was the one that gave him the strength to pull away.

Christian released her and stepped away. When Emory's lids slowly opened, they stared at one another. Understanding flickered in her eyes, but it didn't make his decision any easier. Without a word, he hurried out the front door and down the stairs. Emory's footsteps clanked behind him.

"Christian," Emory called from the porch.

Keep walking. Unfortunately, the command didn't

make its way to his brain soon enough. He stopped but couldn't bring himself to face her.

"Look at me," she said. When he didn't, she repeated her request, "Look at me, Christian, please."

"I can't," he tossed over his shoulder. "I…" He sighed heavily. "…*can't*," he said in a mumble.

"Do you love her?"

He could hear the emotion in Emory's voice and imagined tears streaming down her cheeks. The image cut him to the core. With balled fists, he said, "Don't—don't ask me that, Emory."

"Do. You. Love. Her? It's a simple question. Do you—?"

"*Yes!*" He swallowed the painful lump in his throat. "Yes… I love her." With that, he made haste to his vehicle, slid behind the wheel, crank the engine, and was gone.

The entire drive to his grandmother's house, he played one scene over and over in his head: Emory's mouth inches from his. He struck the steering wheel and a pain shot up his arm. But it was nothing compared to the one that'd tore through his heart as he stood in Ms. Anne's yard and lied to her daughter about loving another woman.

Christian sat in the vehicle a moment to get his thoughts together. He was already an hour late; what would another ten minutes hurt? He'd already earned himself a lecture on punctuality. Taking a few deep breathes and pushing what'd taken place between him and Emory to the back of his mind—for now—he exited the vehicle.

When he entered his grandmother's house—an eight bedroom, ten bath mansion—he regretted not cancelling. Could he really entertain a lecture right now? No. Not tonight. Every hint of energy he'd possessed had been used to walk away from Emory. Could he stay away? That was the million dollar question. God, he felt so trapped, caged like a bird just wanting to be free.

"You're late," his grandmother said behind him. "And no call."

The woman was as light on her feet as a ballerina. He rotated to face her. "I apologize," he said, kissing her cheek. "My phone died."

She cocked a brow. "*Really*?"

As always, Amelia St. Claire was her usual suspicious self. Christian beamed at the pecan-toned woman, flawless from head to toe. "Is POTUS joining us for dinner?"

"If the president were, I'd be awfully embarrassed at the tardiness of my grandson. This is something I expect from Chauncey, not you."

Chauncey and their grandmother had always been like oil and water. He imagined it was because no matter how hard she'd tried, she'd never been able to quite control Chauncey as she had Christian. And it wasn't so much that she was able to control Christian, he simply found it less taxing to occasionally give in than to constantly wage war with her. She didn't go down without one hell of a fight.

"Again, I apologize. I lost track of time," he said.

"Very well. Come. Let's eat. I had Toliver keep dinner warm."

Inside the grand dining room, Christian pulled out the chair for his grandmother. Once she settled, he took a seat next to her.

"I really dislike when you do that," she said.

"Do what?" Of course he already knew what she referred to.

"You know what. Don't play dense with me. I dislike when you sit there. You should take your place at the head of the table, opposite me."

"That was grandfather's seat. Besides, I like being close to you."

At the right angle, one could consider the twitch at the corner of her lips a smile, something she did infrequently. Though she hadn't always been so serious.

Over dinner, they shared small talk: his settling into North Carolina, the construction of St. Claire Aeronautics, the wedding. The latter caused Christian to lose his appetite.

"What's wrong? Is the duck not to your liking? I think it's delicious."

"Gram, do you remember Emory Chambers?"

His grandmother placed her fork down heavily, then dabbed at the corners of her mouth with her napkin. "Yes. I remember her."

Christian eyed her for a moment. "You never cared for Emory. Why?"

The woman didn't hesitate supplying an answer.

"Because she wasn't the perfect match for my grandson."

"What you mean to say is you didn't think she was good enough for a St. Claire."

"No. I just didn't think she was good enough for you. Chauncey, maybe, but not you. Anyway, that no longer matters. You're marrying a lovely girl whom I happen to adore. One who is *quite* suited for you."

Christian was certain the only reason his grandmother *adored* Yasmin so much was because of her last name. Like the St. Claire name, the Manchester name carried a lot of weight and held status. And if there was one thing his grandmother flourished on, it was status.

"And speaking of your bride, she misses you. Which is why I've had the jet fueled and a flight to Dubai arranged. You leave tonight. I'll have the driver take you to the airport."

Christian laughed. "What? Surely, you don't expect me to just pick up and fly to Dubai. Besides, if Yasmin missed me so much, she would be here instead of seventeen hours away."

"She's a supermodel, Christian St. Claire. A highly sought after supermodel at that. You should be thrilled that she is in such high demand."

"Ecstatic," he said dryly, downing the rest of his white wine.

"Dessert now, ma'am?"

She waved off her butler. "No, that won't be necessary. My grandson is leaving. He has a plane to catch."

Chapter 8

Emory tried her damndest not to think about Christian, but she was failing miserably. She hadn't heard anything from him since their exchange in her mother's yard. Three days ago. As silly as it sounded, every time her phone rang, she hoped it was him. How pathetic could she get?

Remembering their last night together, she stabbed a hydrangea into the centerpiece she was working on. The only person she could be pissed at was herself. How could she allow her feelings to take control of her like that? Why did she have the right to question Christian's love for Yasmin? Of course he loved her. He was marrying her for Christ's sake.

"*Yes, I love her.*"

The words rang in her ears like deafening church bells, and it suddenly became difficult to breathe. She closed her eyes and wished that it was all a dream. That

Christian had never strolled into her shop. That she'd never spent time with him. That's she'd tossed the keys back to the rental car agent when he'd showed up at her front door three days ago, stating Mr. St. Claire had arranged the rental of the vehicle for her. She simply wanted to go back to the night before Christian. When things were much simpler.

In a few weeks, it'll all be over, she reminded herself. She would never have to see Christian St. Claire again. The idea brought only minimal relief. As much as she didn't want to see him, the more she craved to see him.

Pathetic.

The shop door chimed, and Emory welcomed the distraction. "I'll be with you in one moment."

Moving from the back of the shop, Emory stopped dead in her track. Of all the people she could have ever guess would visit her shop, Christian's grandmother was not one of them. Her visit could only constitute trouble.

"Ms. St. Clair?"

"*Mrs*.," she corrected her. The woman examined Emory as if she were a reject from a mental institution and wasn't worthy of breathing the same air as her. "Dear, I thought I'd made myself clear two years ago when I asked you to stay away from my grandson."

The woman hadn't asked, she'd ordered. Clearly, Amelia St. Clair had discovered she and Christian had reconnected. But how? Surely, he hadn't told her. Then it hit her. Yasmin had to have mentioned her name and Mrs. St. Claire had put two and two together. Oh, God.

Did this mean Yasmin knew also? Was that the reason Yasmin hadn't responded to the email she'd sent earlier?

"I'm not sure what you believe is going on, but I can assure you anything between Christian and I is strictly business."

"*Really*?"

Emory understood immediately that it was a rhetorical question so she didn't bother answering it. Mrs. St. Claire scrutinized her surroundings with a distasteful scowl on her face. The woman made Emory feel like a visitor in her own shop—an unwanted visitor at that.

Mrs. St. Claire thumbed a poinsettia leaf. Without the courtesy of eye contact, she said, "Stay away from my grandson, *Ms*. Chambers. Since we've had this conversation once before and now again, I trust we won't need to have it a third time?"

She eyed Emory with a look of contempt. Emory folded her arms across her chest but remained silent. If she parted her lips now, something cruel would escape. Even though she loathed the hateful woman, Emory had been raised to respect her elders.

"I'll take that as a yes." She adjusted her chocolate-colored full-length mink coat. "Merry Christmas." Then turned to leave.

Just like the cruel woman to add condescending mock. "I'm not afraid of you. I allowed you to intimidate me then. Not now." Emory wasn't sure where the burst of confidence surfaced from, but refused to back down.

Mrs. St. Claire performed a slow rotation toward Emory, then smiled in a cold, menacing manner. "Silly girl. You should be afraid." Her face hardened even more. "Do you truly believe my grandson still loves you?"

"Yes, I do."

A mix between a smirk and a smile slid across her face. "Well, why don't you just call him and ask. He's at the *Armani Hotel*. In Dubai."

Emory felt a tug in her chest. *Dubai*? That explained why she hadn't heard from him.

"It's such a romantic place. The Armani. You can stand on the balcony and bask in the splendor of Dubai." She glanced at her watch. "Which I imagine he and his lovely fiancée are doing at this very moment." Amelia fished inside her purse, removed her cell phone, then offered it to Emory. "Shall we call?"

Emory's regret shifted to anger. "You are evil. I hope you—" She stopped, refusing to allow this bitter woman any power over her. "Please leave my shop."

"Gladly." She turned and strolled away. "Oh, and in case you're deluding yourself and choose *not* to heed my warning, I'll be forced to tell my grandson that your love of money was far greater than your love for him. I'm sure I don't have to remind you of the fifty thousand dollar check you asked for."

Emory trembled with fury. Through clinched teeth, she said, "I never asked you for a dime."

"Asked. Offered. Does it really matter which terminology is used? You took it. How would you explain that to my grandson? Do you think he'd be so forgiving when he learned your greed outweighed your love?" Mrs. St. Claire cupped her gloved hands. "Good day, Ms. Chambers."

***

Christian hated international travel. The time zone switch, the cultural shock, the distance. But this trip needed to be made. This trip would order every step he took going forward. He rapped on Yasmin's hotel suite door and waited. When he didn't get an answer, he knocked again. Maybe she'd stepped out. Just then, he heard shuffling inside.

"Coming," she said.

When the door opened, she jolted from his presence. Her long, jet-black hair cascaded over the white robe she wore. "Christian?"

"Surprise. Can I come in?"

She stepped aside. "Of course you can."

Inside, he scrutinized the impressive looking room, its modern furnishings, and sleek layout. This was definitely five-star accommodations.

A slow smile lit her face, and she draped her arms around his neck. "It's good to see you. If you'd told me you were coming, I'd have met you at the airport. What are you doing here?"

"I needed to see you," he said. "Face-to-face."

Yasmin pulled away and stared at him, confusion playing in her expression. "Face-to-face? Is everything okay?"

No. Things were far from okay. And he would take the blame for them being that way. Washing a hand over his lips, he pointed to the sofa. "Can we sit?"

By this time, Yasmin's expression had turned to worry. "I don't want to sit, Christian. What's going on? Are my parents okay?"

"Yeah, yeah. Everyone is fine."

She rested a hand over her chest and exhaled heavily. "Thank God."

"Yasmin…" Christian searched for the precise words. "Do you remember me telling you about the time I nearly burned the house down when I was a kid, with Chauncey inside?" He'd never been more frightened in his life when he thought his brother would perish because of him.

Yasmin studied him a moment. "No."

Of course she didn't, because he'd only shared the traumatic experience with one person. Emory. That's how he'd known he loved her. He hadn't been afraid, or ashamed, to show his vulnerability in front of her. He continued, "What about the reason why I wanted to design airplanes?"

"I don't—"

"What about how I felt when my mother died. Or how angry I was at my father when he decided to move to England and start a new family, leaving me and Chauncey for my grandmother to raise? Or why I—?"

"Christian!" Yasmin spoke with her hands. "No, you've never told me any of those things. What is this all about?"

"It's about…love." He paused a moment. "It's about love. I can't marry you, Yasmin. I can't marry you because, in my entire life, I've only ever loved one woman."

These had to be words no woman wanted to hear weeks from her wedding day. He prepared to be mauled, or at least, slapped tasteless. Ignoring the potential risk, he continued. "You have to believe I never meant to hurt you, Yasmin. I just never expected to—"

"To discover you'd never stopped loving Emory?"

Instead of fists, the blow he'd experienced came in the form of words. The shockwave of her comment coursed through his entire body. "How…?"

"I'd misplaced my passport. In the process of tearing up the house looking for it, I came across a box in the garage. I saw pictures of you and Emory together. You looked…happy. Really happy."

He knew exactly the box she referred to. The one he hadn't been able to bring himself to toss out. "Why didn't you say anything?"

Yasmin hugged herself and slid her attention away from him. When her focus returned, she said, "I wanted to at first. I wanted to be angry. I wanted to feel something, anything. But I didn't. I'm pretty sure I should have been livid, but instead, I felt relieved. I think in the back of my mind I was hoping that the two of you would discover you'd never stopped loving each other. It would have given me a way out."

"A way out of what?"

"This engagement. I don't want to marry you either, Christian. I just didn't know how to tell you. Plus, my mother and your grandmother were both so excited. I didn't want to disappoint them."

Christian should have been insulted, upset, or at a minimum hurt. But he wasn't any of those things. Like Yasmin, he experienced relief. And humor. He laughed, then laughed some more. Yasmin joined in and they laughed together.

Sobering, she shook her head. "God, we're pitiful."

"Yeah, we are."

"How'd we allow it get this far, Christian? Neither one of us wanted to be married—at least, to one another. How did it get this far?"

"A lack of communication," he said.

"Yeah. We were never good at that, were we?"

He shook his head. "No, we weren't. Out of curiosity, why did you say yes to my proposal if you didn't want to get married?"

"For the same reason you proposed."

The baby.

Christian rested a hand on the side of his neck. "Funny how things work out, huh?"

"Yes." Yasmin patted her hand against his chest. "You're a good man, Christian St. Claire. Emory is lucky to have you."

Emory. He frowned, doubting she wanted anything to do with him at this point. But that damn sure wouldn't stop him from trying to change her mind.

Chapter 9

Cleaning was what Emory did when she was stressed, and the visit from Amelia St. Claire the day before had stressed her plenty. But something told her Jordyn would have preferred to have been anywhere but inside Emory's walk-in closet, helping to sort through the clutter. Maybe it was the frequent heavy sighs, or the constant trips to the bathroom that lasted fifteen minutes.

Jordyn tossed her head back in frustration. "Can we please take a break?"

"The pizza should be here shortly. We'll break then."

Jordyn blew out another heavy sigh, not bothering to mask her boredom. "Okay."

"You're the one who volunteered to help me, remember?"

"Yes, I did. I just didn't think you'd take your

Christian frustrations out for four consecutive hours. On a Saturday night, nonetheless," she whispered.

Emory laughed. "No one's thinking about Christian St. Claire. I was fine before he strolled into my shop, and I'm fine now." Though, that was hardly the case. "Pass me that sandal. I think I just saw the match in that pile over there."

Jordyn passed Emory a black, strappy shoe. "He loves you, you know?"

Emory stared at Jordyn a moment, then shook off the sting of her words. Christian didn't love her. He loved the woman he was about to marry. Lifting a purse, she said, "Do you want this *Louis Vuitton* bag? It's practically new."

Jordyn pushed the bag away. "That's not a Louis, that's a Stuey. Anyway, did you hear what I said?"

Emory ignored her. "I think I have the wallet to match around here somewhere." She sorted through another pile.

"Emory?"

"Where did I put that wallet?"

"Emory! Stop!"

Emory hurled a bedroom slipper she'd fished from a pile. "What, Jordyn? What do you want me to do? Admit that I love him, too? I do. I love him like I've never loved any man." Lingering tears stung her eyes. "Do you want me to admit that his getting married hurts me to my core? It does, because I should be the one he's pledging forever to. But I screwed up." She exhaled. "I screwed up. Instead of standing up for the man I loved, I walked away from him. His grandmother was right. I didn't deserve him then, and I don't deserve him now."

"His grandmother?"

A tear slid down Emory's face. Dragging her hand across her cheek, she said, "I lied. I lied to Christian. I lied to you. I lied to myself."

"Lied? What does that mean?"

"It means the only reason I broke up with Christian was because of his grandmother. She'd said…" Emory closed her eyes, swallowed hard, and recited the words Amelia St. Claire had spoken to her. "She'd said her grandson was accustomed to having the best of everything. Including women. That I may be a good lay, but that's all I'd ever be to him. '*He's a St. Claire. St. Claire men don't marry beneath them. When he's done getting what he wants from you, he'll dump you like garbage.*'"

The words still packed as much punch now as they had when they were first said to her. Emory decided to spare Jordyn the details of how Mrs. St. Claire had used their mother's diagnoses against her. When the pain from the memory passed, Emory opened her eyes. Tears ran down Jordyn's face, and a great deal of compassion shone in her eyes.

"You never told me," Jordyn said.

"I never told anyone. I… I just wanted to forget."

"Why did it matter what *she* thought? Christian loved you, Em."

"I know he did. But he had dreams, Jordyn. Big

dreams. Dreams that required money. His grandmother threatened to cut him completely off. And I have no doubt the vengeful woman would have. She'd promised he would regret the day he ever met me. I couldn't... I couldn't allow that to happen."

Jordyn slapped at her tears. "You tell him. You tell him now what that...that...*ooo*! I'm so pissed."

"I can't."

Jordyn's face contorted. "You can't? Why the hell not?"

The doorbell chimed, drawing both their attentions.

"The pizza's here," Emory said, eager to end the conversation.

"I'll be right back," Jordyn said, fanning her eyes. "This conversation is *not* over."

But Emory needed it to be. Instead of debating, she nodded and returned to tackling the disarray around her.

After fifteen minutes had passed and no Jordyn, Emory figured she'd escaped to the bathroom again. "Jordyn?"

No answer.

"Jordyn?" she called out again, this time with a bit more authority.

"Jordyn left."

The sound of the masculine voice startled Emory. She gasped at the sight of Christian filling the doorway. His presence made her nervous and caused her heart to pump overtime. Coming to her feet, she said, "Wh—"

The words stuck in her throat.

"What am I doing here?"

She nodded.

"I needed to talk to you."

So many emotions washed over her. Christian's presence was like a breath of fresh air, but it also made it hard to breath. She couldn't continue this way. "You shouldn't be here, Christian." Tempted to ask him about his trip to Dubai, she resisted. That would mean she had to explain how she knew he'd traveled there.

"This is where I want to be," he said.

Stepping over scarves, purses, and shoes, she brushed past him. "I can't do this."

His brows furrowed. "Do what?"

"*This*. Me pretending I can be your friend. I can't. I am in love with you. I've always been in love with you. And because of that love, I'm a sinking, Christian. Every minute we're together, I plunge deeper and deeper. I'm drowning." Tears stung her eyes. "I can't do this. It's not fair to you. It's not fair to me. It's not fair to Yasmin."

"You're right," he said.

Christian took a step toward her, but she warned him off. "No. Go, Christian. Leave, please. Marry Yasmin. Have a house full of babies. You deserve to be happy."

He ignored her plea, moving test-your-will close to her. Cradling her face between his hands, he said, "You're right again. I do deserve to be happy. *You* make me happy. No other woman can do what you do for me. No other woman."

Everything moved in slow motion, or it could have been the speed of light. She wasn't sure. The second his lips touched hers, her mind went numb. He kissed her cautiously at first. Exploring, teasing, filling her with desire.

It wasn't long before his passion grew, both their passions grew. The heat of his mouth sparked a flame that ignited her entire body. She melted a little more with each stroke of his tongue. He offered so much and she unapologetically accepted it all. Greed drew her closer to him. Hunger kept her there.

It'd been two years since she'd been kissed like this. Two years since she'd been kissed by him. Both at once were overwhelming, but she'd weather the devastation to her system if it meant enjoying this a second longer. Christian snaked his fingers up the back of her neck and entangled them in her hair. Holding her head in place, he deepened their kiss.

She wanted him unlike anything she'd ever wanted before. Her heart cried out to him, her body cried out for him. Her soul simply cried because it knew this had to end.

"This is wrong, Christian," she said against their joined mouths. "This is so wrong. You belong to someone else."

"I belong to you. I've always belonged to you."

His words tore through her fog of desire. Resting her hand against his chest, she pushed away from his spellbinding mouth. Her lips ached from the intensity of their kiss. "What are you saying?"

Christian dragged a finger down the side of her face. "I'm saying I couldn't marry another woman when I'm completely and absolutely in love with you. I'm saying I'd risk my own life—in the deepest waters—to save you from drowning. I'm saying let me to be your *life* preserver."

He searched her eyes as if attempting to gauge how his words had affected her. Oh, they'd affected her. So much so that she wasn't sure she'd heard him correctly. "You ended your engagement?"

"Yes."

For some reason, panic set in and she backed away from him on shaky legs.

Christian reached out and hooked her around the waist. "Oh, no, you don't. Don't run from me now." Nestling her against his chest, he said, "Tell me what you're thinking."

How pissed Yasmin must be. Of course, she only said it in her head. Out loud, she said, "You said you loved her."

"I'm sorry. I said what I had to say to be able to walk away from you that night. If I would have stayed, I would have made love to you in a thousand different ways."

She chortled. "I think I would have had some say so about that." She wiggled out of his embrace. "How do I know you're not saying what you need to say now?"

"I've never played with your feelings, Emory. I won't start now?"

What in the hell had he believed he'd done a few nights ago? "You shouldn't have cancelled your wedding, Christian. Especially because of me."

"I didn't do it for you, Em. I did it for me. For the first time in a long time, I'm crystal clear about what I want. And I want you. No one else."

"And you're a St. Claire, which means you always get what you want, right?" She regretted the words the minute they'd slipped past her lips. Why was she allowing his grandmother's venom to poison her thoughts about Christian? She knew the man in front of her, better than most. And he was sincere.

Christian's brow furrowed. "Where did that come from?"

When his cell phone rang, Emory breathed a sigh of relief. "You should take that."

He shook his head. "There's nothing more important than this moment." He rested large hands on either side of her neck. "You love me and I damn sure love you. Nothing else matters. I don't care about what happened in the past. I just know I want you in my present and my future."

"You say you don't care, but—"

He rested his thumb over her lips, then dipped close to her mouth. "I can't lose you again. I won't lose you again."

He captured her mouth, kissing her like a man deprived. His strong arms held her close. Her nipples beaded, the space between her legs throbbed. Her need grew to hunger that craved to be nourished.

Christian abandoned their kiss, but apparently had a change of heart because he recaptured her mouth. He grunted and freed himself again. "Get dressed," he said.

Get dressed? She'd kinda hoped for the opposite. Get *undressed*. He'd ignited her. The least he could do was extinguish the blaze. "Where are we going?"

"We've only been apart two years. Don't tell me you've forgotten."

Two years equivalent to a lifetime. She raked her brain in an attempt to decipher what in the heck he was talking about. "I'm lost," she admitted.

"How could you forget our Christmas tradition? I'm hurt."

Understanding kicked in and she grinned. "The sleigh ride." Which was actually a horse-drawn carriage fashioned to resemble a sleigh. Sentiment flooded her. "*You* remember?"

When they were together, trotting through downtown had always been one of the things she looked forward to most during Christmas. Wrapped in his warm arms and not a care in the world.

"Of course I remember. You're embedded in me, woman." He pecked her gently. "Plus, I have to get you in the Christmas spirit."

She liked that notion. A smile crept across her face. "Give me ten minutes."

***

The second Christian landed back in North Carolina

he'd given his driver Emory's address. Once they'd arrived, Christian had given him instructions to wait because he wasn't sure how things would play out between him and Emory. He'd hoped for the best. He glanced over at Emory. And he'd gotten it.

Splaying his fingers, Emory rested her hand in his. After a short drive, they arrived at a private airstrip. The expression on Emory's face was priceless—a mix of delight and confusion.

"What is going on, Christian?"

"A new beginning, a new tradition. Well, kind of a new tradition. Sorta a twist on the old one."

Emory laughed. "Quit talking in riddles."

"A sleigh ride in Central Park."

Her mouth gaped, then a wide smile touched her lips. But a beat later, she frowned. "New York? I can't go to New York, Christian. My mother—"

"Is in good hands. I've worked it all out with Jordyn."

Her brows crinkled. "Jordyn? When?"

"At your place. Right after she threatened to cut my balls off and feed them to me if I continued to toy with your heart."

Emory slapped her hand over her mouth and muffled a laugh.

"I deserved that," he said. "Your sister doesn't bite her tongue. But I like the way she protects you."

When the driver opened the door, Christian saw a glint of hesitation in her eyes. "Your mother will be fine."

"It's not that." She paused. "The pizza man. We left before he came. I'll never be able to order from there again."

Christian laughed. "We'll call from the air and tell them something urgent came up."

Emory inhaled and exhaled slowly. "New York?" She bit at the corner of her lip. "Okay."

The flight took a little over an hour. Once they landed, they took a cab to the Horse-drawn Carriage Company in Central Park South.

"Our chariot—er, sleigh—awaits," said Christian, extending his hand toward a black, white, and red partially covered carriage. The horse—all white with a red pom-pom atop its head, and bells draped around its neck—was gorgeous.

Moments later, they were nestled beneath a Christmas inspired throw, which did a surprisingly good job at keeping the icy temp from turning them into popsicles. For the next hour and a half, they trotted through Times Square, oohed and ahhed at the breathtaking decorations of the Fifth Avenue shops, enjoyed the display at Rockefeller Center, and marveled at the sheer beauty of Saint Patrick's Cathedral.

"This is nice," Emory said, snuggling even closer against him.

Christian's teeth chattered. "Yeah, it is."

She laughed. "I never understood why you put yourself through sleigh rides. You hate the cold."

"But I love you. And the smile that spreads across your face always warms me nicely."

Emory stared into his eyes, then smiled.

"See, I'm good and toasty now."

"I love you, Christian."

When she frowned, he grew concerned. "What's wrong?"

She leaned against him again, this time resting her head on his shoulder. Something heavy weighed on her mind.

"I feel guilty being here with you, Christian. I keep thinking about Yasmin and how hurt she must be. Just twenty-four hours ago, you were engaged to be married. Now, you're here with me."

Christian placed a finger under her chin and tipped her head so that he could look into her eyes. He contemplated sharing with her the fact that Yasmin hadn't wanted to get married either. Instead, he chose to keep it to himself. He knew Emory. Her first thought would be that he was only there because of it, which couldn't be any further from the truth. He was here with her because this was where he was supposed to be.

"Let me shoulder that guilt. You did nothing wrong. I should have ended things with Yasmin months ago."

"Why didn't you?"

He eyed her for a moment, then turned away. "The night of the miscarriage..." He began again, "The night of the miscarriage we were supposed to attend a charity event. I was running behind schedule. Work. I snapped at her for being so impatient." He sighed. "She stormed out of the bedroom, lost her footing on the stairs. Emory, I'm the reason we lost our child."

Emory rested her hand on his cheek. "No, you're not, Christian. Accidents happen. And that's exactly what that was. An unfortunate accident. But it wasn't your fault."

He'd told himself that a thousand times, but it still didn't make it any easier. "I'd convinced myself I could be content with Yasmin, then I walked into your shop... The second I saw you, I remembered how it felt to be truly happy. I lashed out at you that day in your shop because I was so angry at myself for still loving you after two years."

Emory tilted her head and smiled up at him, then puckered her lips for a kiss. He was more than happy to oblige.

She snuggled against him again. "This skyline view is amazing."

Being here with her was amazing. "Are you comfortable? Not too cold?"

"Perfect," she said.

So was he.

Once they'd finished their tour with a loop around Central Park, a cab whisked them to *The Plaza Hotel*. Not wanting Emory to think he expected anything from her, he opted for a two-bedroom suite. It was the gentlemanly thing to do. "You can have your pick of whichever room you'd like," he said, as Emory moved about the main room.

She faced him slowly, a hint of confusion on her

face. "Okay."

A second later, she recovered and flashed a smile. One he deemed forced.

She pointed. "I…I guess I'll take that one."

Her reaction peaked his curiosity. Had she wanted to share a room with him? Was he taking things unnecessarily slow?

"I think I'll go and freshen up a bit," Emory said.

"Okay. I think I'll take a cold shower—" *Damn*. "Hot shower. I'm going to take a hot shower. Thaw out."

The atmosphere between them mimicked an awkward first date. He wanted to kiss her but knew he wouldn't be able to stop there. Not with the way he craved to be deep inside of her. *Patience*, he told himself. Heck, when they'd first met, she'd made him wait four months before having sex. He'd survived then. Granted, he'd almost gone insane, but survived nonetheless.

Christian shredded the cloak of silence. "Afterwards, we can grab room service. Or go out. Cull & Pistol at Chelsea Market is amazing."

She shrugged. "Either sounds good."

When he nodded, she walked away. The sway of her hips put him in a trance. Once she'd disappeared through the bedroom door, he shook his head. Damn thawing out. He needed a serious cool down.

Chapter 10

Emory hadn't enjoyed the hot shower as much as she normally would have. Not with things so weird between her and Christian. His awkward behavior caused a thousand scenarios to play in her head. The most troubling—him having second thoughts about being there with her.

It didn't make sense. He'd kissed her at her place with such intensity it'd left her breathless. Then they'd been cozy and affectionate during the amazing carriage ride. Now, he acted as if he were afraid to touch her. And separate bedrooms? What'd happen between then and now?

Okay, she understood him not wanting to rush into a sexual relationship, but they could at least hold each other, right?

Thinking about what she'd just said to herself, she laughed. *Hold each other*? She laughed again. There was no way she could intimately snuggle with that man and not want to make love to him. Especially with the insane way her body responded to his touch.

Fastening a towel around herself, she stared at the huge, empty bed and shook her head. An eerie reminder of the past two years. Pondering that fact, something rushed over her. No way was she spending tonight alone. She'd suffered too long without Christian.

Emory entered Christian's bedroom and posted at the window. When he exited the bathroom, she faced him just in time to see the surprised expression crawl across his face. Still in her towel, she strolled toward him in a slow, seductive manner. "I changed my mind. I think I like this room better. It has an amazing view of central park."

Christian eyed her for a moment, then his lips curled. "That's too bad, because I've grown quite fond of this room. I don't think I want to give it up."

"*Hmm*. Then it seems we have a problem."

"Appears so. How do you suggest we solve it?"

Emory's eyes slid to his mouth, then seared a trail down his damp torso. A line of fine black hairs disappeared beneath the towel he wore. Finding his eyes again, she sucked her bottom lip between her teeth.

A look danced in Christian's eyes... Potent. Primal. Promising. Without a doubt, the next few hours would be ones she would enjoy. Answering her body's plea, he placed his hand in the gather of her towel and pulled her toward him. A beat later, his mouth covered hers.

Winded, Christian pulled away. "I need to make love to you. I know you probably want to take things slow and I respect that. So, I'll wait if you say I have to. And I'll do it with patience. But I want you, Emory. I want you so bad it hurts."

She'd always been good at giving him what he wanted. Without uttering a word, she loosened the gather of her towel, allowing it to fall into a puddle on the floor. It was time to see who wanted whom more.

Her body had changed over the past two years. Breasts that once stood at full attention weren't as pert. A once flat stomach now had a small pouch. Thin thighs were thicker than they used to be. But she loved every inch of her body. And by the way Christian's crotch tented his towel, so did he.

He drank her up with his eyes. "Damn. I don't think a female body could be more beautiful than yours." He glided a finger over her shoulder, across her collarbone, and down the center of her chest. "Every inch. Beautiful."

The sensation from his touch caused her words to come out in a clumsy mess. "You were engaged to a supermodel. I'm definitely not that."

"There's something a supermodel can never be. Something no woman could ever be."

Emory moistened her lips. "And what's that?"

He rested a hand on the side of her neck. "*You*. Tonight is all about you. About your every want. Your every need. Your every desire."

"I *want* this moment to be about more than

pleasure. When we make love, I *need* you to know I'm returning a part of myself to you I snatched away. My every want, my every need, my every desire…is *you*. I love you like no other, Christian St. Claire."

Christian walked her backwards until the back of her legs touched the bed, then guided her flat onto the mattress. Emory held his eyes until he broke contact, knelt, and kissed along her inner thigh. Her body sizzled each time his lips touched her scorching flesh.

Delicate kisses peppered the thatch of curly hairs on his journey to the opposite thigh. Each time he made contact with her skin, she grew more and more anxious. Why was he torturing her? He had to know how much she wanted him, needed him, craved him. As if he'd sensed her urgency, his warm mouth claimed her core.

Instant sensations tore through her, causing every muscle in her body to twitch. If she experienced this kind of reaction now, her body would surely short-circuit and shutdown when he brought her to an actual orgasm.

Christian spread her further apart, using his tongue with the skill of a trained marksman, who aimed right…on…target. He hadn't lost his touch, bringing her to a climax in record time. Emory's back arched off the mattress. Her nails made a zipping sound as she dragged them across the bedding. There was no taming the intense waves of pleasure crashing through her, so she didn't try.

The kisses Christian planted on her as his body inched up hers only intensified the sensations already claiming her. He sucked one of her hardened nipples between his lips and teased it with his tongue. A deep moaned flew past her lips when his hand settled between her legs.

"Yes," she whispered, when his fingers curved inside of her. She ground her hips into him, wanting...needing deeper penetration.

"I can't take it another second," Christian said, stopping abruptly.

For the next few seconds, everything was a blur: Christian undressing, sheathing himself, and blanketing her body with his.

Sated, Emory smiled. "That was—"

"Delicious," he said, finishing her thought with his own narrative. "And only the beginning. Kiss me," he whispered close to her mouth.

Lifting her head, she welcomed his mouth against hers. His tongue snaked past her lips, and she sucked it gently. All of her focus had been on the kiss, until he slid his hardness inside her. A whimper escaped as she molded around him. He still fitted her perfectly.

"That's a beautiful sound." His mouth hovered at her ear. "I've missed you," he whispered and nipped her lobe. "I've missed hearing you moan when I'm inside you." He kissed her jaw. "I've missed the way your body responds to mine and mine to yours." He pecked her gently on the lips. "I love you, woman. And I want to spend all night inside of you, making you come until your body begs for mercy. Is that all right with you?"

"Absolutely. But don't be so sure it'll be my body

begging for the mercy."

With that, Christian drove into her hard and deep. The sound she emitted would surely prompt the neighboring rooms to contact security. Obviously, he was determined to dominate her. One delicious stroke at the time.

It wasn't long before the tingle of another orgasm gripped her. She dug her nails into Christian's moistened flesh as fire raged through her. The intense release snatched her breath away.

Christian's strokes slowed, grew clumsy. If she had to guess, he neared his breaking point. Two or three strokes later, he shattered, releasing a guttural noise that mimicked more a growl than a moan.

Collapsing down next to Emory, he pulled her into his arms. Winded, he said, "Don't get too comfortable. We have a long night ahead of us."

***

Emory had been awake for hours, simply watching Christian sleep. His partially opened lips allowed soft snores to escape. If someone would have told her a year ago—heck, a week ago—she'd be laying here with him, she would have called them a liar. Yet, here she was. Happier than she'd been in months.

With the tip of her index finger, she traced along the lips that'd given her hours of intense pleasure. Christian didn't budge. He'd always been a hard sleeper. "I love you, Christian St. Claire," she whispered into his ear. "You're my Christmas wish come true. I'll love you 'til the ocean runs dry." It was something they used to say to one another.

She kissed his cheek, inched out the bed, and headed for the bathroom. Like the rest of the suite, it too defined luxury. Gold faucets, mosaic tile, glass, marble. She'd bet the cost of this room could make a nice dent in her debt.

After emptying her full bladder, she decided to take a shower. This time, she enjoyed the feel of the water caressing her body like heated fingers. After what seemed like an eternity, she stepped out and wrapped herself in one of the robes provided by the hotel. The supple fabric felt as if she'd been swaddled in a cloud. The only other thing that felt this good against her was Christian.

When she exited the bathroom, she'd half expected Christian to be awake, but he was still fast asleep. At four in the morning, she should have been, too. Instead of returning to the bed, she made her way into the ridiculously enormous living room.

Retrieving the iPad from the glass-top cocktail table, she adjusted the lighting and the temp. When her stomach growled, reminding her she hadn't had dinner, she raided the in-room refreshment center, then prepared a cup of hot tea.

Moseying to one of the numerous windows, she glanced down at the bustling city. Even at this early hour, people moved about. *This truly was the city that never sleeps*. She rested her hand against the icy glass as if to feel the heartbeat of The Big Apple.

"There you are."

Before Emory could turn, Christian wrapped her in his arms.

Nuzzling the side of her neck, he said, "Couldn't sleep?"

She shook her head.

"What's on your mind?" he asked, kissing the side of her neck. "Whenever there's something eating at you, you can't sleep."

Clearly, he still knew her quite well. There was so much she needed to tell him. Things that could derail their happily ever after. Rotating in his arms, she said, "What do you think your grandmother will say about...about...*us*?"

He chuckled. "Is that what's bothering you? What my grandmother thinks?"

Not really, but she nodded anyway.

His expression grew serious. "I'm my own man, Emory. My grandmother doesn't dictate who I can and can't love."

"She's never liked me."

"But I love you. That's all that matters. That's all that has ever mattered. That's all that will ever matter. My grandmother doesn't have to love you because I do. She does, however, have to respect you."

Respect from Amelia St. Clair. Not likely. But the notion brought a smile to her face. One that would have lasted longer had she not recalled the fact his grandmother still had the upper hand. "Christian, I

116

need—"

"*Shh.*"

Christian removed the cup from her hand, took a sip, then placed it on a table. Grabbing one of the tails of fabric holding her rob together, he gave it a gentle tug. A second later, the robe fell open. For the first time since he'd been there, she realized he was buck-naked. The sight sent a jolt of excitement straight to the space between her legs. They desperately needed to talk, but her arousal took precedence.

"You were saying you needed something." he said, kissing her neck.

Oh, he was tricky. Emory hummed a sound of satisfaction. "You," she said in a heated breath. "I need you."

"You got me," he said, inching the robe off her shoulders and kissing her skin. "You've got me. 'Til the ocean runs dry."

Chapter 11

Emory hated saying goodbye to New York but was happy when they touched down in North Carolina. There was truly no place like home. And though NYC was a fun place to visit, she wouldn't want to live there. It moved entirely too fast for her.

"You ready?" Christian asked, extending his hand for her to take.

"Yeah, I guess."

He wrapped her in his arms and nuzzled his face against her neck. "Say the word and we can jet anywhere you'd like."

"*Mmmm*. As tempting as that sounds..."

What she'd miss most about New York wouldn't be the delicious food or the extreme experience of Christmas. It would be the carefree feeling she'd had while there, wrapped for countless hours in Christian's arms. In his arms, there were no overdue bills, no threat of losing her business, no constant worry about her mother. Most of all, there was no Mrs. St. Claire with her scowls and threats.

Mrs. St. Claire.

Thinking about the woman dampened her jovial mood. But the idea she'd spent the weekend making love to the bitter woman's grandson restored her happiness. Unfortunately, the buoyant feeling only lasted a short time because there were still things she needed to share with Christian.

Emory groaned to herself. When Mrs. St. Claire found out about their excursion—and Emory was sure she would—would she go through with her threat and risk exposing her part in the whole thing? It only took Emory a second to answer. Yes, she would. Why had Emory even questioned that? And it was Amelia St. Claire, which meant she would find a way to come out of it squeaky clean. Why did the woman hate her so much? All Emory had ever done was love her grandson to the fullest.

Dispersing the dark cloud hovering over her head was the only way they could move forward. "Christian, I need to tell you something," she said in a rush. Now seemed like as good a time as any to tell him everything. Plus, the details were best coming from her, because Mrs. St. Claire would surely put a twist on the facts.

"Can you tell me in the car? It's so cold out here," he said. "I need some of your warmth."

Emory squealed when he pulled her into his arms.

Rolling in laughter, she said, "You're such a cold weather wimp."

He squeezed her butt. "Wimp? I'll show you a wimp tonight."

She looked forward to it, if they made it to that point. There was still the matter of the conversation they needed to have. The thought renewed her urgency. "Yes, we can talk inside the car."

The driver stood by the waiting vehicle to open the door, but Christian dismissed him. She laughed as Christian playfully pinned her against the car, the icy cold penetrating the layers of her quilted primaloft coat. His mouth lingered inches from hers, thin plumes of fog escaping.

He rested his forehead against hers. "This is going to be the best Christmas of my life."

"Why?"

"Because I have you."

It was exactly what she'd hoped to hear.

He held her face between his hands. "And this time—"

"You two are going to catch your deaths out there."

The familiar voice froze them both.

Christian thawed first, pulled away, and glanced toward the open window. "Gran? W..." He glanced at Emory, then back to his grandmother. "What are you doing here?"

Emory realized she'd been holding her breath and released it in a long, steady stream. Unable to blink, the bitter wind burned her eyes. Mrs. St. Claire's presence put her in a state of utter shock and confusion.

Mrs. St. Claire's probing eyes settled on Emory. "I thought I'd welcome you two love birds back to town."

Even with the frigid December air, Emory felt the burn of her heated glare. The confident expression on her face told Emory there would not be a pleasant end to the beautiful weekend she'd shared with Christian.

"Emory, you remember my grandmother?" Christian asked.

"Yes," she said, barely audible. Oh, but how she wanted to forget her. *Pull it together, Emory*. The worst thing you can do now is show weakness. *Stiff chin*.

Stone-faced, Mrs. St. Claire said, "Please, get inside."

Emory wondered how difficult it'd been for her to say please. Even with its use, the request felt more like an order than an invitation. But if, in fact, it were an invitation, it was more than apt for Emory to decline. Walking had to be better than what would surely go down inside the vehicle.

Christian placed his hand on the small of her back and urged her forward. Her hesitant steps dragged across the asphalt. The temperature inside the vehicle was comfortable but seemed to increase the second Emory settled against the leather next to Mrs. St. Claire—making herself easy prey for the lioness.

"Comfy?" Mrs. St. Claire asked.

Not even close, but Emory nodded anyway. She wanted to peel out of the suffocating coat. Maybe no one would notice the barrier of sweat she felt around her hairline.

What was Mrs. St. Claire up to? The not knowing was killing Emory—slow and uncomfortably. Just the fact that the woman was being cordial was enough to keep Emory on high alert. CONTENTS UNDER PRESSURE flashed in her head. This situation was bound to explode at any minute.

Emory toyed with a few scenarios in her head, none of them good. Maybe she should just confess everything right now, foil whatever cruel plot Mrs. St. Claire had conspired.

"I take it the two of you had a grand time in the city. It is lovely this time of year. Wouldn't you agree, Emory?"

Christian touched Emory's hand and she flinched. What'd happen to all of the courage she'd processed when Mrs. St. Claire had visited her shop? Her words were caught in her throat, but thankfully, Christian answered for her.

"We had a great time. I think we'll make it an annual tradition."

He squeezed her hand and she smiled nervously.

"That sounds like a grand idea," said Mrs. St. Claire.

Emory knew the comment had to infuriate her, but the woman did a great job of concealing her distaste. *Any minute now*, Emory kept repeating to herself. Any minute the top on this boiling pot would blow off.

What kind of game was being played? Obviously, Mrs. St. Claire knew the wedding had been called off, because she hadn't voiced her objection about the two of them being in New York together. Who'd dropped the bomb on her? Yasmin or Christian? Shamelessly, Emory would have loved to have seen the look on her face.

Emory nonchalantly checked her watch. Would she ever make it home? The sooner she removed herself from the scornful woman's space, the better. When they finally pulled into the driveway, Emory breathed a sigh of relief. When Christian stepped out of the vehicle, Emory turned to Mrs. St. Claire. "Please don't," she pleaded in a hushed tone.

Mrs. St. Claire turned away and stared straight ahead as if Emory hadn't spoken a word. How could anyone be so heartless? Especially at Christmas.

Outside the vehicle, Emory pushed the door closed behind her and rested her hands on Christian's chest. "Are you coming inside?"

He kissed her gloved fingers. "In a second. I need to speak with my grandmother a moment."

Emory's stomach knotted and churned. "O...okay." She stared up at him, wanting, needing to say more, but the words escaped her.

A look of concern spread across Christian's face. "Are you okay?"

"I..." She shook out of her stupor. "Yeah, everything's fine. I'll see you inside, okay?"

He smiled. "Yes, you will."

She tried to move away, but he captured her by the waist.

"When I get inside, I intend to debunk that wimp comment. Be ready."

Under normal circumstances, his words would have turned her on and made her giddy with anticipation. Not this time.

Each step away from the idling vehicle filled Emory with more and more dread. Her stomach did back flips and her temple felt as if she were being drilled in the head with a dull bit.

Inside, she paced back and forth, then moved to the blinds and attempted to peep through the tiny slits where the cord strung through. Unable to get a clear view, she parted the slats ever so slightly, and just in time to see Christian moving toward the house.

She couldn't get a read on his expression from this distance. Two taps sounded at the door. Taking a deep breath, she trudged across the floor. The second she pulled the door open, the broken look in his eyes told her he knew everything—or at least the version his grandmother had wanted him to hear.

When her eyes lowered to the paper he held, Christian offered it to her. Emory's chest tightened the second her eyes settled on the image of the cancelled check his grandmother had written her two years ago.

"I wanted to tell you, Christian. And it's not what you think."

Christian ran a hand over his head and glanced around in a confused manner. The pain she witnessed in his eyes when they finally narrowed on her ripped her heart to shreds.

"Every time my grandmother told me you were only after my money... I defended you. I defended you because I believed that what we had was real. That you loved me for me and not for what I could do for you."

"And I did, Christian. And *I do*. I never—"

In a raised tone, he said, "You never what, Emory? Cared about my money? Meant to hurt me? What?"

"Both."

"Yeah, well, that check tells a different story."

That check told lies. Emory fought to remain levelheaded, convincing herself that his cold tone was a result of his hurt. In his shoes, she'd probably react in a similar manner. Plus, the evidence did support what he clearly believed to be the truth. "It's not how it looks."

"Is that your signature?"

He already knew it was. "Yes."

"You cashed the check?"

Again, he already knew the answer, but she played along. "Yes."

"So, it's *exactly* how it looks."

"Christian, look me in the eyes and tell me you truly believe I was with you for your money. Do you truly believe—?"

"You know what I truly believe, Emory? I truly believe you should have asked for more. You damn sure deserved it."

He made a move to turn, but stopped when she grabbed his arm. When he snatched away, she didn't believe her heart could break any more. But it did. "Can't you see what this is all about, Christian? It's about your grandmother working any angle she can to keep us apart. You can't be that blind to her motives."

Christian scoffed, turned, and descended the stairs. When he stopped at the bottom, she thought maybe, just maybe, he'd considered what she'd said about his manipulative grandmother.

Facing her, he said, "Your mother wasn't recalling a scene from any movie. I had asked for your hand. The night you ended things, I'd planned to propose." He paused. "I guess I should consider myself lucky that you never gave me the opportunity. I would have given you anything, Emory. *Anything*. All you ever had to do was ask."

With that, he crossed the yard, entered the waiting vehicle and was gone.

***

The second the vehicle backed out of Emory's driveway, Christian felt as if a part of his heart had been snatched away…again. His focus remained out the window. So many emotions battered him: Anger. Hurt. Confusion.

Yeah, he was confused as hell because it made no sense that Emory would take money from his grandmother. But she'd stood right in front of him and admitted it, so what was there to be confused about?

A vision of Emory's sad eyes played in his head

and, for a brief moment, guilt flooded him. Shaking the feeling off, he pressed his lids together tightly and massaged the pain in his neck.

"Grandson—?"

Christian held up his hand, and his grandmother stopped mid-thought. He'd heard enough from her to last him a lifetime. "I can't. Not now." She touched his arm, and he pulled away.

"I understand," she said softly.

Did she? Could she? How could anyone understand the pain he felt without being inside of him? He allowed his head to fall back against the headrest. *Fifty thousand dollars*. That was all he'd meant to her? A lousy fifty thousand dollars.

Had she lied about how she'd gotten the money to open her shop? *Small business loan my ass*. Clearly, she hadn't considered the fact that it would take more than a mere fifty thousand dollars to run a successful business.

When his cell phone rang, he fished it from his pocket. Emory's name flashed across the screen. For a brief second, he contemplated answering. But what could she say to him that would undo what she'd done?

Sliding his thumb across the screen to send the call to voicemail, he stashed the phone back in his pocket and returned to his closed eyes position. He fought the images of Emory laying beneath him, smiling and claiming to be happier than she'd been in years. One thing for sure, she was damn good at being convincing.

"I spoke to Yasmin," his grandmother said. "You

called off the wedding?"

So much for leaving him to his thoughts. Clearly, Yasmin hadn't owned up to not wanting to get married either. He imagined his grandmother eyeing him, waiting on a response. One that would never come. He didn't want to discuss a wedding—or lack of one. He didn't want to discuss Yasmin. And he damn sure didn't want to discuss Emory.

She continued, "Why would you—?"

His cell phone rang again. This time he didn't bother removing it from his pocket. The ringing gave him a reprieve from the sound of his grandmother's voice.

"As I was saying—"

"Why?" Christian said. He could feel his grandmother shift toward him.

"Why, what?"

When she'd painted the vivid picture of Emory's deceit, he'd gotten the feeling she wasn't telling him everything. He opened his eyes and studied her. "Why would you wait all of this time to tell me this? Why did you keep it from me, period? I deserved to know."

"I kept it from you because I knew how much it would hurt you." She fumbled with the black leather gloves draped across her lap. "If fifty thousand dollars was all it took to—" She stopped abruptly. "It was money well spent. I'd do anything to protect you and your brother. Back then, you thought you were so in love with the girl. I was protecting you."

"I was in love with her." He instantly regretted the

roughness of his tone. Despite the circumstances, he would never disrespect his grandmother. Calming, he said, "You didn't want to hurt me then. Does that mean you believe it's okay to hurt me now?"

Her expression hardened. "I *believed* I was doing you a favor. I've shown you the kind of...*woman*—and I use the term loosely—you were dealing with. The kind of *woman* you abandoned a perfectly good mate for. Shouldn't I get a thank you instead of your unappreciative attitude?"

"Stop the car," Christian said, through clenched teeth. His door swung open before the vehicle came to a complete stop.

"Where in heaven's name do you think you're going?"

"I'll walk. I need to clear my head." He slammed the door. The window lowered as the vehicle moved alongside him.

"Christian St. Claire, are you insane? We're more than twenty miles from the manor. Do you plan to walk the entire way? And through this neighborhood?"

"I really need to be alone right now."

"You're sulking over that woman? After everything I've told you? How pathetic. Drive!" she ordered the driver, the window rising.

The car disappeared in the distance. Christian came to a stop. His jaw tightened, and he pulled his gloved hands into tight fists. A beat later, he released all the frustration he harbored through a tortured sound that seemed to echo for miles.

Chapter 12

Emory tried Christian's cell phone once more. The fifth time that day. She'd given him space and hadn't tried to contact him since the debacle three days ago. And of course, he hadn't reached out to her either.

When his voicemail answered, she left another message. This one would be the last. "Christian, it's me again. Emory," she said, as if he wouldn't know or had forgotten her already.

"I know you don't really want to hear from me. Evident by the unreturned calls. Please, give me this one last thing and I won't ask anything else of you. Just give me the opportunity to talk to you face-to-face. The opportunity to explain. Please. I deserve that much."

She hated sounding so desperate, but in a way, she was. She could respect him wanting nothing more to do with her, but she wouldn't allow him to believe money had been the reason she'd walked away. And she was sure his grandmother had painted her as greedy and loveless. Neither was true.

"I'll be home after six. I hope you come. I..." She debated her next words. "I love you, Christian. I always have."

The second she ended the call her phone rang. When her mother's name scrolled across the screen, she grew concerned. "Hello?"

"Emory?"

"Mom, what's wrong?"

"Nothing, sweetie. I had Ifede dial you. You couldn't sleep last night. I just wanted to check on you."

Clearly, her mother was having one of her good days. She'd referred to Ifede by her actual name and not *that pretty girl with the bright eyes*. "I'm sorry if I kept you awake last night, Mom."

She'd spent the night with her mother. Sleep had evaded her, so she'd spent most of the night tossing, turning, and pacing the floor. She contributed it to the fact that she wasn't in her own bed but knew the real reason. *Christian*.

"You didn't keep me awake. I'm a night owl. You know that."

They both laughed.

Her mother continued, "You know what that means, don't you? When you can't fall asleep at night."

That I have entirely too much on my mind.

"It means you were awake in someone's else's dreams."

She doubted that to be the reason. "I'm glad you

called, Mom. I always love hearing your voice."

"I need to tell you something else," her mother said.

"Okay." There was a pause that worried her. "Mom?"

"Trust God through this storm, baby. He'll never let you down."

Emory's eyes filled with tears. Even going through her own battle, her mother still found the strength to encourage and support others. "Thank you. I really needed to hear that."

"I know you did, sweetie. I'm your mother. I know these things."

With her voice cracking with emotion, Emory said, "Well, do you know how much I love you?"

"Oh, yes, I do. I know it by the way you care for me. In love, actions speak so much louder than words. Know that I love you, too. We'll talk later."

Emory wiped at her eyes as she pulled the phone away from her ear. The shop door chimed and, for an instant, she got excited from the notion it could be Christian. But it was only Jordyn.

Emory sighed. "*Oh*. It's just you."

Jordyn rested her hand on her hip. "Well, great to see you, too, sis."

"A small part of me hoped you were Christian." A much larger part than she was willing to reveal. Maybe she should just let him move on with his life. Maybe this was fates way of intervening, telling her she didn't deserve to be happy. But why? She and the universe had had their ups and down, but what in the hell had she done to fate?

"Still nothing?" Jordyn asked.

Emory shook her head. "Still nothing."

Jordyn rested a hip against the metal table and folded her arms across her chest. "You have to see it from his perspective, Em. He believes you chose money over him. He's pissed and upset. Once he comes to his senses, he'll realize what the two of you share is real."

Shouldn't she be the one pissed? Shouldn't she be the one upset? He'd walked away without even looking back. She stilled. Hadn't she done the same to him? Was this payback? Emory sighed heavily.

Jordyn draped her arms around Emory's neck. "Don't worry, he'll come around."

"He won't even give me the opportunity to explain. Don't I at least deserve that much?"

"You could go to him," Jordyn said, apprehensively.

Emory's shoulders slumped. "I don't know. He's not taking my calls. Would he open the door if I showed up at his place?"

Just then, the door chimed again, drawing both their attentions.

"*Oh, it's just you*," she and Jordyn said in unison to the parcel delivery man.

"And a Merry Christmas to y'all, too."

"Sorry, Irvin," Emory said. "You know I'm always happy to see you. It usually means a fresh flower delivery. What woman doesn't love receiving flowers?

Even when she is a florist."

"No flowers this time," he said. "All I have is this. From…" He squinted at the writing. "Johnson, Jones & Jones Law Office."

Emory wrinkled her brows. "A law office?" A bad feeling rushed over her. Was one of her creditors suing her? After signing the device he offered, she accepted the large envelope. Tearing into the package, she removed the documents inside and read them carefully to herself.

"What is it?" Jordyn asked, glancing over Emory's shoulder.

Emory thumbed to the second page. "It's…" The air in the room thickened, and she found it difficult to breath. She slapped her hand over her mouth, steadied herself on the edge of the table and passed the pages to Jordyn. Allowing her hand to fall, she said, "Why would he do this?"

Jordyn scanned the documents, then glanced up at her, a wide smile curling her lips. "Because he loves you, Em. This man loves you."

Their mother's words echoed in Emory's head. *In love, actions speak louder than words*. She reclaimed the pages—one a deed to her shop, the other the deed to her mother's house—and scanned them again. "They're dated over a week ago," she said. "Before Christian and I even—" She stopped mid-thought.

"*Screwed*?" Jordyn said with a smirk.

"Watch your mouth." Emory removed her apron. "Will you watch the shop for an hour?"

"Of course I will." Jordyn shooed her away. "Go. Get your man. Don't forget your phone. I'm going to need you to call me with details."

Emory retrieved her cell phone from Jordyn. "Thanks." It rang before she could slide it into her purse. She considered allowing the call to roll into voicemail, but a call from Nadia Chandler—one of North Carolina's premiere wedding planners—usually meant lucrative business. Hitting the speaker icon, she placed the phone on the table and slid into her coat. "Hi, Nadia."

"Emory, please don't strangle me, but remember the message I left you about the St. Claire/Manchester wedding?"

Yes, she remembered. She'd been in New York with the ex-groom at the time. "Yes."

"Ignore it. The wedding is back on. This couple is going to be the death of me."

The air seized in Emory's lungs, and she pushed her lids together to stop the room from spinning. Her stomach cramped and bile burned her throat. She found the corner of the table just in time to stabilize herself. But a second later, her legs turned to jelly and she crumbled to the floor.

***

If the banging on Christian's front door was any indication, his door would fly off the hinges soon. What in the hell was going on? And who the hell was hammering on his door like the police?

When he flung the door open—using less caution than he should have—Jordyn barreled past him, waving a pair of shears identical to the ones he'd used at Emory's shop. "Jordyn, what the hell?"

She pointed the tip of the blades at him. "Do you remember what I said I'd do to you if you didn't stop toying with my sister's heart?"

He instinctively shielded his crotch. "I'm going to return her calls. I just need—"

"When? After your honeymoon?"

Christian's head snapped back in surprise. "Honeymoon?"

"You swore to me that you loved my sister more than anything on this earth. You're a fucking liar, and I'm going to castrate you. Let's see how you manage on your wedding night without a dick."

When she lunged for him, he grabbed her and held her in a reversed bear hug. Wrangling the shears from her, he said, "First, watch your mouth," because that's what Emory would have said. "Second, what in the hell are you talking about?"

Jordyn squirmed to free herself. "Don't play dumb with me, Christian St. Claire. Your wedding planner called. She said the wedding is back on." She squirmed more. "Let…me…go."

The news struck him like an iron fist to his stomach. He knew sure as hell he hadn't changed his mind about marrying Yasmin and vice-versa. So what—? *Gran*. The woman had definitely overstepped this time.

"I'm not getting married, Jordyn. And I didn't lie to you. I do love your sister. With all my heart."

Jordyn stomped on his foot with the pointy-toed shoes she wore. He grunted but held firm to the grip he had on her.

"If you don't let me go right now..."

"Not until you calm down and listen."

"Like you listened to my sister when she tried to tell you your grandmother is a spawn of the devil?"

Before he could respond, she snaked a hand free, reached behind her, and placed his balls in a kung-fu grip. "*Oh, Sweet Jesus,*" he said in a tone that would be the envy of any opera singer.

When he was ten, he'd been hit in the head by a foul baseball. The pain didn't compare to the agonizing hurt he experienced now. His knees buckled, crumbling him to the floor in a fetal position. He swore he'd lost consciousness on his way down. Stars and birds floated around him. Through clenched teeth, he said, "I'm...not...*getting married.*"

Jordyn hovered over him, showing little regard for his agony. "Then why did your wedding planner call the shop and say you were, huh?"

He growled at her. "I don't know, but I'm sure my grandmother had something to do with it."

"Your grandmother?"

"Yes."

Jordyn seemed to soften, as if his explanation made sense. She knelt beside him. "Can...I get you some ice or something?" She flashed a nervous smile, morphing back to the pleasant person she usually was.

"I swear to God, if I didn't love your sister so much, I'd have you arrested."

"Wouldn't that be overkill?"

"Get out."

"I'm sorry, Christian. I snapped. Haven't you seen that show?"

"*Get...out.*"

"You won't mention this to Emory, will you?"

"Get out! Get out! Get out!"

"Okay, okay. You don't have to be so dramatic." She hurried to the door, but stopped shy of exiting. "If it makes you feel any better, now I understand why my sister walked funny when you guys returned from New York. You're packing some heat."

He hurled a remote across the room.

"Bye, Christian. Love you."

As soon as he got the feeling back in his legs, he was up and out the door. A short time later, he exploded into his grandmother's front door. He strayed from his normal routine—straight to the kitchen to raid the fridge—and instead, moved through the house in search of her. "Gran! Gran!"

Gran stood at the top of the spiraling staircase. "Have you lost your mind? I haven't seen or talked to you in days. Now you come in screaming like a madman?"

Climbing the stairs, he said, "Did you call the planner and tell her the wedding was back on?"

"Why, yes, I did," she said nonchalantly. "I figured

that once you came to your senses, you'd realize the mistake you've made."

"Gran, I've never disrespected you, and I won't start now. But there will be no wedding. I love Emory. Do you hear what I'm saying to you? I. Love. Emory," he repeated. He pounded his chest with a closed fist. "With everything within me. And you know what else? I don't care about the money she took. I love her beyond her faults."

"You don't care?"

"No."

"Then that makes you a damn fool." She descended the stairs. "Love is overrated."

"How can you say that? What happened to you, Gran? What happened to the woman who used to waltz in the rose garden with Grandfather? The woman who used to serenade him with love songs? The woman who showed me what love looked like by the way she loved her husband. What happened to the woman who would have celebrated my and Emory's love?"

When his grandmother stopped in the middle of the hallway, he stood in front of her. "I love Emory, and I'll say it a thousand times if that's what it takes for you to understand that. Gran, one of the many reasons why I love her is because in some ways, she reminds me of you."

She scoffed. "And how exactly is that?"

"She's stubborn and full of pride." He ignored her scowl. "And she loves me. I don't care what you want me to believe. I know Emory loves me."

"Really?" His grandmother glanced away.

"If she'll have me… If she'll forgive me… I'm going to be with her, Gran. I want Emory in my life. And honestly, I don't have a life without her."

"You did have a life. A wonderful life. With Yas—"

Exhausted, he said, "Yasmin didn't want to get married, either, Gran. We were trying to force something not designed to fit. We were suffering. Emory freed us both."

By the expression on her face, something about his words shook her. Maybe she'd realized he wasn't backing down on this.

"Emory is a part of my life. A huge part of my life. I hope you will accept this. I need you to accept this. But if you can't…" He shrugged, turned, and moved away, leaving her there to fill in the blank.

Chapter 13

Emory answered the door on the second chime. When she saw Christian standing there, it wasn't joy or pain she felt. It was defeat. She just couldn't take any more.

"Hey. Can I come in?"

After a long, tense-filled moment, she stepped aside.

Once in, he turned to face her. "I'm not marrying—"

Emory flashed a cautionary palm. "I know. Jordyn told me." She'd also mentioned that she'd probably ruined Christian's chances of ever fathering kids.

"I don't care what happened in the past, Em. I don't care about the money. I just want to be with you."

"You do care, Christian. If you didn't, you would have been here before now. And you have the right to care and to hear the truth. Your grandmother—" She stopped abruptly, staring deep into his eyes. Pain still lingered in them. As much as she wanted to reveal every cruel and hateful word his grandmother had spewed at her to cause Emory to end their relationship, she couldn't. She refused to hurt this man any more than she already had.

"My grandmother, what, Emory?"

Though Mrs. St. Claire was as lethal as a king cobra, Emory knew she loved Christian in her own twisted way. In good conscious, she couldn't do anything to destroy their relationship. The truth would most certainly do that. If he were okay with the past being the past, so was she. "Loves you. Your grandmother loves you."

Before Christian could respond, the doorbell rang.

Emory rested a hand on the side of her neck, still not believing she'd protected Amelia St. Claire. The woman who'd made her life a living hell. "It's Jordyn. We were going out to dinner."

"Make sure you pat her down for any sharp objects. You may not know this, but your sister's a little crazy."

Emory chuckled at the expression of genuine concern on his face. The second she pulled the door open and saw her visitor, she gasped. "Mrs. St. Claire?" Emory refused to go another round with her. What was she doing there anyway? Hadn't she done enough damage?

"Gran?" Christian inched Emory away from the door as if he expected his grandmother to tackle her. "What are you doing here?"

"May I come in?"

The woman's tone was soft and kind, but from experience, Emory knew this was simply the gentle breeze before the hurricane. Christian glanced to Emory for approval. When she nodded, he stepped aside.

The usually callous woman didn't regard Emory's house with the same disdain she had the shop. In fact, she didn't take a single glance around. Emory was eager to learn why the matriarch had gotten down off her high horse to stand in her living room.

Mrs. St. Claire eyed Christian. "I owe you an apology. And you, as well," she said, facing Emory. "Especially you."

Mrs. St. Claire apologize? Emory waited for the cameraman and crew to jump out, because she was sure she was being pranked.

"Admittedly, I'm not the easiest person to like or love. And sometimes, I need to be put in my place. Earlier, my grandson did just that." She refocused on Christian. "He called me out. He asked what'd happened to me." She paused a moment. "After your grandfather died...I abandoned all memories of love, including how it felt to truly give and receive it. Instead, I welcomed grief, loneliness, despair. It slowly turned me into a bitter woman."

Amelia St. Claire showing vulnerability? *Any minute now*, Emory thought. This had to be some kind of prank.

"Today you reminded me so much of your grandfather. A great, great man. He would have been proud of you, but appalled and ashamed of me."

When Mrs. St. Claire smiled, it stunned Emory. She'd actually smiled, and her face hadn't cracked.

"Your great-grandmother did not care for me to be in your grandfather's life. The daughter of a maid and a field hand wasn't good enough for her son. I was beneath him, she'd once told me."

Emory bit at the corner of her lip, reliving the moment Mrs. St. Claire had said something similar to her.

Mrs. St. Claire continued, "But your grandfather and I were determined to be together. He sacrificed everything to be with me. I saw that determination in you today. You were willing to sacrifice for the woman you love."

What had Christian done? What kind of sacrifice had he attempted to make?

Mrs. St. Claire turned her focus to Emory. "I've said some horrible things to you. Have done even worse. I've lied and manipulated you both."

Emory cradled herself in her arms and willed her tears not to fall. In a thousand years, she'd have never imagined this callous, never yielding woman exposing herself like this. "It's okay."

Mrs. St. Claire shook her head. "No, it's not."

To Christian, Mrs. St. Claire said, "I'm the reason your relationship ended. I did to this young lady exactly what your great-grandmother did to me. The only difference, she loved you enough to keep it from you. I imagined she knew it would ruin our relationship."

Christian eyed Emory. "Tell me this is not true."

When she remained silent, he turned away from them both.

"Jesus," he said.

As much as Emory wanted to run to him, wrap him in her arms, she held back.

"I know I've hurt you, grandson. At the time, I believed I was doing what was best for you. When I forced the money on her, I'd learned—"

Emory intervened. "Mrs. St. Claire, you don't have—"

"Yes, dear, I do."

Christian slowly turned to face them. "When you *forced* the money on her?"

"Yes. She never asked for the money as I stated. I'm ashamed to admit this, but I'd learned of her mother's diagnoses of Alzheimer's. I told her if she loved you, she wouldn't burden you with it. That you were doing great things and this would only be a distraction. I told her how expensive it would be to care for her mother on a secretary's salary and that I could help. I bent her until she broke."

"*Jesus*," Christian repeated.

"I could have said no," Emory said, surprising herself by coming to Mrs. St. Claire's defense.

"No one can says no to my grandmother. She doesn't process the word." Christian rested his hands on either side of his neck, closed his eyes, and shook his head. "You could do that to me, Gran? You could do that to your own grandson? You knew how much Emory meant to me. You knew—" He choked with emotion. "You knew and you did it anyway." Opening his eyes, he said, "Who are you?"

Tears glistened in the broken woman's eyes. "I'm so sorry. I'm so sorry. I don't want to lose you. I can't lose you. You and your brother are all I have. I'd die if..."

Tears streamed freely down Emory's face. To watch this unfold was both heartbreaking and beautiful. Beautiful because she was seeing a side of Mrs. St. Claire many would never get to see, or believe existed.

"How can I forgive you for this, Gran?"

"The same way you were willing to forgive me," Emory said. "When you came here tonight, you were prepared to forgive and forget the past for me. You have to do the same for your grandmother." Emory turned to Mrs. St. Claire. "I forgive you. I never wanted to come between the two of you. All I ever wanted to do was love him."

Mrs. St. Claire nodded, clearly struggling to keep her tears at bay. "Looks like we do have something in common. Our love for my grandson. I'm sorry I made your life a living hell. Hopefully, in time, you'll discover I'm not the wicked witch I appear to be."

Emory wasn't sure anyone on earth had enough time to debunk that theory.

After a moment, Christian took his grandmother in his arms and held her tight. "I love you." Kissing the top of her head, he said, "We'll talk later."

Mrs. St. Claire smiled. "I'd like that." To Emory, she said, "Thank you."

Emory smiled and nodded. It felt good to take the highroad.

When Christian returned from walking his grandmother to the waiting town car, he cradled Emory's face between his hands. "How could you ever believe I wouldn't have loved and supported you through your mother's diagnoses? Why didn't you tell me what my grandmother had done? Why—?"

Emory placed her index finger over his lips. "Kiss me. Kiss me like it's the first time you've ever touched my lips."

"I spent two years without you, Emory. Two years that—"

"Kiss me like you're making up for the twenty-four months we were apart."

Christian chuckled—a smooth, sexy sound that caressed the deepest part of her soul.

"Is this your way of shutting me up?"

She rested her warm hands on his cheeks. "Yes, it is."

Christian wrapped his large hand around her neck, but he didn't apply pressure. Something about the move warmed her entire body like a shot of fine whiskey. His hand coiled to the back of her neck, then glided upward until his fingers tangled with her hair. Fisting her locks, he guided her head back gently. His mouth dipped low and hovered over hers. The heat escaping from his mouth aroused her like a gentle touch to her most sensitive areas.

"Don't ever walk away from me again, woman," he

said.

"I won't," she said, eager to taste him.

He searched her eyes. She hoped he found whatever he was probing for soon, because the waiting to explore him was driving her insane. A smirk played at the corner of his mouth. Yep, he'd found it.

He captured her mouth and kissed her as if the world was minutes from ending and he wanted his delicious pain to be the last thing she felt. She wrapped her arms around his waist to keep from losing her balance—revealing just how powerful and intense the kiss was.

Christian's hot breath against her cheek grew heavier and heavier, mimicking her own rugged breathing. If by chance the world had ended, she would have gone a very satisfied woman.

In theory, this could actually be labeled the twenty-four-month kiss because that's how long it appeared it would last. The deep satisfying exchange made her feel as if she were floating. Then it hit her, she was floating. Into Christian's arms. When he'd lifted her off the floor, her legs wrapped instinctively around his waist.

Christian lowered to the carpet, Emory holding tight. Finally abandoning her mouth, he lifted his head and stared down at her. She witnessed so much strength, so much truth, so much love in his eyes it took her breath away.

"My life restarted the second I stepped into your shop," he said in a whisper. "If anyone would have ever told me I could love another human being the way I love you, I would have called them a liar."

A tear ran out the corner of her eye, and Christian kissed it away. His tenderness caressed her heart.

"Close your eyes," he said.

When she did, he kissed both lids. The tender act sent a jolt of warmth through her entire body.

"What do you see?"

She laughed. "Darkness."

"Look beyond the darkness."

Searching, she smiled. "I see the first time we met. I see the first time you said 'I love you'. I see the first time we made love."

He chuckled. "*Really*?"

"No. All I see is darkness, Christian."

"That darkness is our clean slate. No heartbreak. No loneliness. No me without you. Just our present and our future with no remnants of the past."

A wide smile curled her lips. "I see it now."

"It's beautiful, right?"

Emory opened her eyes. "Gorgeous."

"A clean slate, Em. Nothing holding us down. Agreed?"

Emory frowned. She couldn't agree. Not until... "I need to share something with you."

Before he could question her, she'd wiggled from underneath him, got to her feet, and held out her hand for him to take.

A look of confusion shadowed his features. "What's going on?"

She could show him better than she could tell him. Leading him into her bedroom, she directed him onto the bed. "I'll be right back." She entered the closet and exited a moment later dragging a coconut-colored chest. Placing it at his feet, she said, "Open it."

Christian arched a brow. "What's in it?"

"The last piece of the past," she said.

With caution, he unlatched and lifted the lid. "Wh...?"

"All fifty thousand. I could never bring myself to spend a single dime of it.

For a moment, Christian appeared to be at a loss for word. Finally, he eyed her. "You've been struggling, Emory. This money could have really helped you. Why didn't you use any of it?"

"Because, in my heart, it would have been like betraying you, betraying our love."

Christian took another glance at the stacks of money, then closed the chest. Pushing to his feet, he stood directly in front of her. "Do you know how amazing you are? How truly amazing you are, Emory Chambers?"

Emory shrugged. "Yeah, I do."

They shared a laugh.

Christian wrapped her in his arms and she snuggled against his chest. "Santa gave me exactly what I wanted for Christmas," she said.

"Oh, yeah? And what was that?"

She tilted her head to eye him. "You."

Christian pecked her lips gently. "Looks like we

both got what we wanted."

Emory fiddled with the scarf around his neck. "Remember when I said I'd pay you back every dime you spent on my car."

His eyes narrowed in questioning. "Yeah."

"Well, would you like that in big or small bills?"

They shared another laugh.

"Didn't we establish I wouldn't accept a dime you offered?"

"You have to. You've done so much for me. My car. Paying off my shop, mother's mortgage. I owe you so much, Christian. Thank you. From the bottom of my heart. You are the amazing one. And I'm eternally grateful to you and for you."

He tipped his head forward and kissed her. "Clearly, I haven't convinced you that I would do anything for you."

Emory smiled. "Yeah, you have. But now you have to do one more thing for me."

"And what's that?"

"Accept this money as repayment." She smiled. "You know I don't like to be indebted."

Christian studied her a moment. "I have a better idea for this money."

Christian reached inside the chest and removed a single twenty dollar bill. He folded and refolded the currency. Tucked here, creased there.

Emory laughed. "Are you making a money airplane?"

A couple of minutes later he was done. It wasn't

an airplane. Cleary, he, too, possessed a few talents she wasn't aware of. "You want to make fifty thousand dollars' worth of origami rings?"

"No. I wanted to make one ring. We'll spend the other forty-nine thousand, nine-hundred and eighty dollars on our wedding."

"On our wed—" When he lowered to one knee, Emory's mouth fell open.

"We've been through a lot. Things meant to break us. But we held strong to our love for each other."

Emory draped her hand over her mouth and nodded, tears stinging her eyes.

"I can't promise you we won't have bad days. I can't promise you that every day with me will be perfect. I can't promise you that I won't make mistakes. What I can promise you is that I'll be your lover and your best friend. That I'll be everything a good man can and should be to his wife. I promise my trust, my loyalty, my devotion. I promise that I will love you fervently and unconditionally 'til the ocean runs dry. And even then, I won't stop loving you. Emory Gale Chambers, will you marry me and make me the happiest man on this planet?"

"Are you sure about this, Christian?"

"I've never been surer of anything in my life."

A tear escaped down her cheek. There was no need for hesitation. She wanted to spend her life with this man. "Yes, yes, yes. I'll marry you."

Christian slid the money ring onto her finger. "A perfect fit."

Emory regarded Christian with admiration. "We're a perfect fit."

When he came to his feet, he captured her mouth in a heady kiss. The idea of a lifetime of kisses like this thrilled her. She protested when Christian tried to pull away.

He dragged a bent finger down her cheek. "They say whatever you're doing when the New Year comes in is what you'll be doing all year long. I want to marry you on New Year's, at the stroke of midnight, because vowing my love to you is what I want to be doing every single day of my life. What do you say?"

"I say...yes."

Emory squealed when Christian yanked her into his arms and spun her around. She owed Santa and apology. Turns out, he'd sent the right man after all.

Thank you, Santa.

THE END

Dear Reader,

I'd first like to say THANK YOU so much for your support! Many of you are spreading the word about Joy Avery romances like wildfire, and I'm eternally grateful! My goal is, and will always be, to continue writing beautiful love stories that take you on an emotional and satisfying journey toward happily ever after. I hope you will stay along for the ride.

I hope you've enjoyed reading THE NIGHT BEFORE CHRISTIAN. Please help me spread the word about Emory and Christian by recommending their love story to friends and family, book clubs, social media, and online forums.

Also, I'd like to ask that you please take a moment to leave a review on the site where you purchased this novel.

I love hearing from readers. Feel free to email me at: authorjoyavery@gmail.com

Until next time, HAPPY READING!

ABOUT THE AUTHOR

By day, Joy Avery works as a customer service assistant. By night, the North Carolina native travels to imaginary worlds—creating characters whose romantic journeys invariably end happily ever after.

Since she was a young girl growing up in Garner, Joy knew she wanted to write. Stumbling onto romance novels, she discovered her passion for love stories. Instantly, she knew these were the type stories she wanted to pen.

Real characters. Real journeys. Real good love is what you'll find in a Joy Avery romance.

Joy is married with one child. When not writing, she enjoys reading, cake decorating, pretending to expertly play the piano, driving her husband insane, and playing with her two dogs.

Joy is a member of Romance Writers of America and Heart of Carolina Romance Writers.

WHERE YOU CAN FIND ME:

WWW.JOYAVERY.COM
FACEBOOK.COM/AUTHORJOYAVERY
TWITTER.COM/AUTHORJOYAVERY
PINTEREST.COM/AUTHORJOYAVERY
AUTHORJOYAVERY@GMAIL.COM

Be sure to visit my website to sign up for my
"WINGS OF LOVE" newsletter!

Made in the USA
Coppell, TX
23 November 2020